ENCHANTRESS

Robin Jackson

This book is dedicated to the love of my life. Without her constant love and support, I would not have been able to do this.

I love you Marilyn.

Forward: Looking Back

Well, it's 2011 and this book, which I conceptualized and wrote in 1991 and 1992 is ancient history. As you read it remember that the Internet was just becoming commercially viable and that Stuxnet was literally 20 years away.

I have purposely avoided rewriting this novel to conform to today's technologies, so what might seem trivial today was only in my mind's eye in 1991.

Also, the statistics and information in the prologue are original as well. Can you imagine the consternation of more than 6,000 viruses written against the Intel platform? Today we are fighting millions of viruses across multiple platforms and their inevitable mutations.

I hope you enjoy the book, and now that I don't have to rely on publishing houses to "get it," I hope to dust Evan and COMPOPS off and give you an update of what they are doing in the cyber domain now.

Enjoy!

Rob

Prologue

Throughout the centuries, intelligence gathering has made its impact upon the course of human events. Whether the historians stumble upon the evidence of such efforts or not is the true test of the prowess and dedication of those who practice the art "sub rosa."

This novel seeks to discern and fictionalize what is theoretically the state-of-the-technology. It is not predicated upon any knowledge of activities by any agency or agencies of the U.S. Government or those of any other government. If I had any such knowledge then this book would not be possible. I am a firm believer in the efforts of the intelligence community, and would not knowingly compromise any intelligence effort.

As technology progresses, so does the art of intelligence. Intelligence collection is the art of gathering information. This information can be derived from open sources as well as from covert operations. Codes, ciphers, secret writings, and their surreptitious reading have been the stanchions of intelligence, along with the tried and true human intelligence. As new technologies have become available, means for collecting information have become more advanced as well.

The value of a collected body of even unclassified works when analyzed and correlated by the practitioners of intelligence analysis can yield conclusions which would be classified if those conclusions were themselves to be contained in a document. When you understand this then the fact that a group of computer hackers in the Netherlands was discovered to have broken in to several unclassified military computer systems in May of 1991 has a different level of import.

Unfortunately, as reported by ABC News, the government of the Netherlands and its academic community actually encourage such penetrations, and there exists no law to punish the offenders.

Recently (1991), a consortium of scientists concluded that the security of computer systems, in general, is far below what it should be. To paraphrase the conclusions of this report - "users of computer systems have been extremely lucky." Perhaps this fictional novel will help to explain the very real threat to lives, business and property, unsecured computer systems pose to our society. For an insight into a real computer crime and the vulnerability of the United States' computer infrastructure I would direct the reader to the exceptional book "The Cuckoo's Egg," written by Clifford Stoll and published in soft cover by Pocket Books.

The wealth of information readily available from computer systems may not be immediately apparent to the uninformed. However, our whole society is becoming one based upon information. Computer systems control our money, our manufacturing, our automobiles. Whether you realize it or not, you are affected by these computer systems on a daily basis. I have extrapolated upon the progresses made in the field of computers to derive this piece of fiction.

This is the story of the fictional heroes who mine information from these new electronic repositories and utilize it to combat the enemies and oppressors of freedom throughout the world. It is also about those who would exploit our lack of awareness about computers to wreak havoc upon society, either as individuals, or as part of an organized effort.

Just as knowledge and awareness of other terrorist techniques can safeguard us from those threats, a strong understanding and respect for the possibility and results of electronic terrorism, can avert that which is otherwise inevitable.

The most publicized incidents of viruses are the annoyance viruses that have proliferated through personal computer systems. Mcafee and Associates, a company which writes virus protection software, has cataloged more than 6,000 distinct viruses and their mutations on the IBM compatible computer system alone! None of these attempts (as far as I have knowledge) has been perpetrated by anything more than the equivalent of computer bullies. The old adage "a little bit of knowledge is a dangerous thing" seems to apply in these cases.

For the most part such virus writing groups or individuals are disdained by their peers, and would be shot on sight if they were discovered (and such an act were allowable in our ever merciful system of jurisprudence).

So I've fictionalized, and added a true malice to the existing viruses. In doing so I had to have a good-guy (at least I thought so). Thus, COMPOPS was formed in my imagination. If there are heroes of the type that are represented by my fictional COMPOPS, then I mean them no malice, and pray that their work goes unhindered and undetected until the end of time. I hope that any such individuals might appreciate my admiration for individuals with the sense of dedication and the talent to perform miracles which make the events in this book look like parlor tricks. I also pray that their judgment is as temperate and upstanding as that of most of the characters in this book, lest such knowledge and ability be perverted.

April 2, 22:45 EDT

The smoke hung pensively around the light of the single brass library lamp. Silence combined with the smoke to complete the spell cast by the 20th century mage. Anticipation mixed with the concoction, making the room unbearable to the uninitiated. The silence taunted the agent code named NECROMANCER. It mocked NECROMANCER's intense desire for the single sound signifying that the spell had taken hold of its victims.

Suddenly, the sound came.

It was the intense high pitched call of a beast seeking companionship in the darkness. Surely, the sound was related to that of the Harpies', able to drive a man mad if allowed to continue for too long. Fortunately, the sound was met and the beast quickly soothed. Satisfied that a suitable mate was found, the noise subsided, replaced by a dance of lights that signaled success.

NECROMANCER tensed as the lights danced the sweet mating dance that the agent knew so well. "Soon," the agent thought, the expectation welling like a geyser.

The agent examined the augury using a modern crystal ball, a computer terminal, waiting for its amber glow to tell of the success of the magician's spell. A cryptic narrative unfolded upon the screen telling the mage all the details of the creature which had been put under the mage's spell.

The spell complete, the lights ceased their mating dance. The distinct click of the telephone disconnecting invited a flurry of activity on the part of the computer in NECROMANCER's study. The data which took seconds to transmit would be encrypted so well that it would take more than 50 years of supercomputer time to decipher it. This was still more magic woven by the mage to protect the secrets of the incantation which had been cast.

NECROMANCER's breath returned. The agent drew deeply from the Marlboro and gave thanks to God for sweet victory. A smile appeared on the agent's face at the sight of the last message, "ENCHANTMENT complete...awaiting instructions." NECROMANCER cleared the computer screen, the blinking amber cursor winked at the agent as if it were acknowledging the remarkable achievement.

The flurry of activity which had just occurred represented the culmination of months of work and planning on NECROMANCER's part, and the part of others. Sitting in the dark study, NECROMANCER reflected upon the toil and risk that had gone into the birth of the ENCHANTRESS program. The planning and design had stretched the limits of the small organization's capacity. The risk that ENCHANTRESS might be discovered before it could serve its purpose made the project that much more tenuous.

NECROMANCER had conceived ENCHANTRESS.

Indeed, NECROMANCER had toiled over the program day and night for months, nurturing it timing it, rewriting it until there was not a single line of program that wasted motion. The program had become like an athlete that trained and trained until every ounce of effort was expended efficiently.

NECROMANCER took distinct pride in ENCHANTRESS. It pained the agent to have to try and explain the significance of the program to the uninitiated. Not knowing the significance of what ENCHANTRESS was programmed to do, nor the efficiency with which the program accomplished its task, those not trained in the black arts could not express the same awe that NECROMANCER was sure would be expressed by another technomage.

Still, NECROMANCER's superiors did express sincere awe, akin to the awe of some ignorant tourist upon seeing the Mona Lisa. They were awed either because they thought they should be or because they had no comprehension of the work of art they were viewing.

NECROMANCER was not put off by this lack of technical appreciation, the agent was sure that soon, very soon, the entire community of mages would be in awe of the ENCHANTRESS program, and the prowess of the magician who had cast the awesome spell upon mankind's workhorses.

Apr 3, 06:45 EDT

Although he had worked late into Sunday night, Evan Smith was on the expressway headed for work by seven. Evan was no stranger to late hours or working on weekends. It was just another aspect of his job. It was an unspoken requisite that civil servants in the intelligence community worked almost constantly. It was considered quite gauche to complain about the hours or the pay. For true intelligence people the reward of the job was not money, it was an internal feeling of accomplishment and service.

The weekend had rewarded Evan greatly. He had worked late into the night downloading information pertinent to the safety of millions of people. To Evan it had been worth the extra effort to bring in what he hoped would be conclusive proof of Iraqi chemical weapons production.

His recent success caused this strapping six foot tall sandy haired lad to beam as he drove down the expressway. He had put some Bob Seager on the CD player, something he liked to do when he was feeling his oats. The wind was blowing through his hair from the open window. It was already 65 degrees and turning into a typical Maryland spring day.

While it was his recent success which had led to his mood this beautiful April morning, work was not on Evan's mind as he headed south down 295. He had learned that the key to maintaining a cover was in living it fully unless he were actually doing "Company" work. It was a forced split personality that helped all good intelligence personnel keep their sanity.

Evan had never really accustomed himself to the thought that he was a "spy." He never left the U.S., never had to endure clandestine meetings. He had never even been taught in the art of self-defense. Yet Evan was considered a "spy" by his peers and his enemies alike. He was a new generation of spy, and a very capable one at that. He was able to obtain the wares of spies throughout the centuries with an alacrity and in quantities unrivaled by his predecessors. Evan traded in information, and the quantities and quality of his wares were beyond compare thanks to his considerable talents and understanding of the machines that men trusted as their confidants in this golden age of technology.

Evan turned off at a nondescript exit in the Maryland countryside, not far from the infamous Washington Beltway.

The average traveler would not be compelled to detour into the rural surroundings which were typical of southern Maryland. None of the local residents suspected the magnitude of the organization which housed itself discreetly in several five story office buildings near the local shopping mall. Yet, only a few hundred feet from the local fast food restaurants and clothes emporiums, the world was being monitored by Evan and his compatriots.

From the unpretentious brick buildings, which were nestled in among the scenic Maryland trees, the heartbeats of nations, friendly and hostile, were constantly checked.

Secrets of friends and enemies alike were subtly pried from the bowels of what were perceived to be secure information systems. These secrets were scrutinized, weighed, categorized and disseminated while mothers checked the fit of their children's new shoes and teens discussed the latest top 40 hits over milk shakes mere meters away.

As he parked his Subaru in front of one of these nondescript brick buildings he tensed mentally for a second. He braced his mind for the never ending pressure that he would face until he departed late in the evening. Another day at a job which didn't exist, working for an organization that didn't exist either.

"Monday," was all he thought, as he locked the car and headed into the building.

The inside of this building was no different than any of the hundreds of other offices occupied by contractors and government agencies alike. Listings for the contractors' offices appeared on the directory. Many of the contractors existed solely to serve the government agencies with whom they were housed. The symbiotic relationship served to boost the economy by an immeasurable amount. The ability to quantify the benefits of the money injected into the economy from these relationships was burdened by the cloak of secrecy which hung over their budgets.

These organizations, masked in a cloak of nonexistence, had nurtured the economy through camouflaged veins and changed the face of the nation with the birth of new technologies developed initially to feed the hidden behemoth known as the intelligence community.

Evan walked to the elevator. He looked around to ensure that no one else was near as he entered.

Once inside he inserted his key into the maintenance lock on the elevator and moved it to an unmarked position. The elevator whirred and slowly moved up to the fourth floor. As the elevator started its tenuous climb, Evan pulled out his nondescript security badge. The simple portrait displayed on the front of the badge was of him. In D.C. these badges were a dime a dozen.

Those in the know would be able to place Evan with the Defense Intelligence Agency (DIA). Beyond that very little could be discerned. This was convenient when Evan had to travel or attend conferences with his peers in the intelligence community.

Except for a small office at DIA with one secretary, who would cover if anyone called, the agency which Evan worked for had no connection to DIA whatsoever. DIA benefited from the agency's intelligence, and the Director of DIA was always happy to over-bill for the small square footage which the agency leased. It was a classic example of the inter-agency relationships which developed in this business.

The real secret of the badge resided in its black magnetic band on the back. This band contained the encrypted data that allowed Evan to enter a world that few humans knew existed, and even fewer people worked in.

The data on the card could only be read by a magnetic card reader which was connected to a sophisticated computer system. The irony of the fact that access to this agency was controlled by a computer was not lost on Evan. Because Evan and the small contingent of other intelligence personnel who worked within the confines of the offices behind the locked doors spent their lives tricking computers into yielding their well-kept secrets.

As the elevator doors opened Evan met the gaze of the security guard. Evan smiled and inserted his badge into the reader. He then entered his eight letter security code. The light on the machine turned green and he withdrew his card. "Damned new computers do most of my work for me," sighed the security guard.

"Yeah, but they aren't marksmen," returned Evan. "I don't think I'd want to give one a gun."

"I know what you mean," said the guard, smiling. "You should have seen what one did to my phone bill last month."

Evan smiled. He sincerely cherished his job and the people with whom he worked. He jauntily headed for the a small steel box mounted on the wall next to the door. It was a mechanical cipher lock which provided further assurance of an entering person's right to pass into the secret world that lay beyond.

Evan placed his fingers into the confines of the box and pressed the four number code that released the final lock. He swung the door open and entered the brightly lit main office of COMPOPS, the government's computer operations organization.

COMPOPS was to computer intelligence (COMPINT), what the CIA was to human intelligence (HUMINT). There was not as much glamor and recognition as working for the FBI, CIA, or even DIA, but that was to be expected when working for a "no-such" organization.

In fact, a large part of COMPOPS' success laid in the fact that no one even suspected its existence.

Although there was no acknowledgment of the agency's existence, the job was no less strenuous, and no less dangerous than CIA work. The identities of the personnel working for COMPOPS were well hidden. The secrets which Evan and his co-workers knew would deal modern western intelligence a fatal blow if revealed.

The easiest way to prevent leaks was to deny the existence of that agency. Further measures were taken, of course, but the most effective weapon was what the intelligence community called "deniability."

That is why agencies such as COMPOPS, which don't officially exist, are known collectively as "no-such" agencies. The more sensitive the information collected by these agencies, or the more intricate the methods used to obtain information, the fewer the people outside of the agency who even knew of the existence of the "no-such."

Less than a dozen people outside of the agency Evan worked for knew of its existence. Less than half of those people knew in any great detail the capabilities of the organization.

Unfortunately, people who have been exposed to such organizations, and who have had no real appreciation for their precarious nature have routinely given the public, and the enemy, glimpses inside of them. These glimpses are as rare as those of the Loch Ness monster. They do nothing to serve the public's edification. But they give the enemy subtle clues which force changes in systems to insure that they remain impenetrable.

With the ever increasing reliance upon computers to store and analyze intelligence, computer systems had become another means by which these secrets could be exposed. Insecure systems were dealt with quickly and severely.

Very quickly the techniques for testing the security of these systems became formalized and the men and women who were proficient in testing them were grouped together to form TIGER teams. These teams' whole reason for existing was to test and ultimately penetrate government computer systems.

More than one complacent computer system administrator had lost his job because of a TIGER team penetration. Because of the adversarial relationship between agency computer administrators and TIGER team members. TIGER team members were seldom offered the lucrative jobs available to the majority of federal computer professionals.

As the TIGER team techniques grew it became apparent that intelligence might be gained from utilizing TIGER teams against foreign "targets." Of course the incursions must be surreptitious. But that's what the TIGER teams prided themselves in. This theory was tested rigorously against a variety of computer systems. Once the techniques had been advanced to the "state-of-the-art" the infiltration was begun.

Evan had helped hone the techniques which became the foundation of the second generation of COMPOPS tools while he was still with the TIGER team. Ultimately, Evan had been persuaded to join several of his companions at COMPOPS where he had proven his abilities time and again.

Evan had no technical peers in COMPOPS. He lacked a little bit of tact, and that had cost him a few points in his career growth. But Evan didn't really want the directorship anyway. He simply wanted to be the best at what he did. According to the few people privy to his work he was unrivaled and that was enough for Evan.

Evan's attention was caught by a tall dark haired, dark complected man in his early forties, Paul Sanders, Director of COMPOPS.

"Evan," Paul called. "I didn't expect you in so early this morning. You put in a long day yesterday. If you don't knock this off we'll never be able to pay off the national debt, just because of your overtime."

"Yeah," responded Evan. "If only I got paid for it. I've got so much comp time coming that I was thinking of taking a two year sabbatical and doing some advanced work at MIT."

"Kid's stuff," replied Paul, laughing. "I'd be afraid you'd start showing them how to do stuff the right way and end up blowing the cover off our whole operation."

"Well...," said Evan, a glint of laughter in his eye.

"Seriously," said Paul. "I just wanted to let you know that Jahmal is here and is ready to start going over those printouts you got from our Iraqi break."

"Great. Do you have that guy from technical lined up yet?"

"Yes," answered Paul. "I got Gary Eagleton to work with you. You know him from that Afghan work we did a few months ago."

"That's good. He really knows his chemicals. If anybody can make heads or tails of this it's Gary."

"That's what I gathered," said Paul. "Gary is getting read on to your projects and should be in later today. Jahmal is in your office already. Why are you sitting here gabbing?"

"Slave driver," returned Evan, as he started for his office. He knew that the obligatory reading and signing of security agreements pertaining to the different "compartments" of information, what was referred to as being "read on", would take Gary a good part of the morning. That meant that he had some time free after he talked to Jahmal and before Gary was ready to get to work.

"Ingrate," laughed Paul.

Evan laughed and headed down the corridor to his office. Because of the compartmentalization of the COMPOPS agency every individual had his own office. This helped reduce the amount of information inadvertently heard by other members of the organization.

While techniques and methods were commonly discussed among departments, the actual intelligence derived from explicit targets, as well as the targets themselves, were not common knowledge.

Evan's office was crowded with books and equipment of his profession. It was here that any pretense of social normalcy could be shed. Evan lived for one thing and one thing alone, to master computer systems. The various books on his shelves were some of the keys to this mastery. The awards which covered the walls bore stark testimony to his prowess.

Many of the awards that Evan had won could not be displayed, however. They were kept in his personnel file, only able to bear testimony to the very few people privileged to the intelligence which COMPOPS provided. Those few people did not need to read the numerous citations, though. They knew the man.

Evan Smith was unpretentious. Born to teacher parents at the University of Montana, in Missoula Montana, Evan had thrived on computers from the earliest age.

As a child he would coo when he was allowed to sit on his father's lap in the den, watching the green characters flash on the screen and listening to the lullaby of the keyboard clicking. As he matured, so had computer technology. By the time he was in high school the most successful computer in the country was the one developed in a garage in California.

Four years later, that particular computer that had been so successful, was a child's toy, and still the industry grew.

Evan received a full scholarship to MIT to fulfill his dreams and upon graduation had been recruited by the Computer Security Center in Maryland. It was at the CSC that he had worked on modern day TIGER teams.

Maryland was a long way from the majestic beauty of Montana. Evan missed that beauty most of all, when he reflected upon his life.

Fortunately, Evan seldom paused for reflection. Evan, after all, was a realist and lived with his feet planted firmly in the present. He occasionally vacationed in Montana when time and the demands of the job permitted. However, he hadn't been back to his home state for more than two years.

He kept in touch with his parents through numerous phone calls and computer correspondence. The latter being his favorite method of interacting with his father. They both shared a love for esoteric computer systems and problems, and had collaborated on several books and programs. Because of Evan's knowledge, each project had to be reviewed by his agency before it could be released. But Evan could very quickly tell where the edge was and made sure to stay far away from it in his unclassified forays.

He valued the work of his colleagues, and the goals of COMPOPS in general. The COMPOPS charter, the framework under which it was organized and tasked, was very explicit and limited in its area of operations.

He knew that there were those that would have him believe that the intelligence community was not needed, and indeed loathsome. However, Evan regarded these people as naive in their understanding of the problem, or the benefit of intelligence work to peace. Had it not been for accurate intelligence the Cuban Missile crisis might have been dramatically different. Accurate and precise intelligence had helped to change what was estimated as being a very long and costly Desert Storm operation into one of the most successful and least fatal military successes known in the history of warfare.

Little did Evan realize how desperately his computer skills would be needed in the coming weeks, nor the sacrifices that would be made to slay the bewitching ENCHANTRESS that was at work, even as Evan himself worked similar magic in the name of freedom.

Apr 30, 23:10 EDT

NECROMANCER touched the portion of the bookshelf that released the hidden bolt. The bookshelf swung inward to reveal the walnut paneled interior of a hidden den. NECROMANCER walked in, closed the door, and turned on the brass library lamp next to the computer system.

NECROMANCER reclined in the leather chair and breathed deeply. The agent was away from the hassles of the boring cover job. The agent no longer had to keep up the pretense of cool professionalism.

Programming excited NECROMANCER.

Penetrating computer systems was like forbidden sex to the agent.

The sheer magnitude of the latest accomplishment had made it nearly impossible for NECROMANCER to continue the cover job. The agent thought constantly of the cleverness of the virus. The virus which NECROMANCER had conceptualized and sold to the plethora of superiors and financial supporters.

NECROMANCER was loosing the ability to sink back into the cover which justified the agent's normal existence. NECROMANCER had not been in the field long enough to realize the error of such emotion. The agent only felt the impending coup and the excitement was intoxicating.

The agent turned on the computer system, and connected the communications gear to the telephone line.

Looking at the digital clock, NECROMANCER withdrew a Marlboro from the box and lit it with a silver Zippo lighter. The agent drew on the cigarette drawing comfort from its warm ember.

The smoke rose into the light. Suddenly, the ritual of lights started as a computer system called into NECROMANCER's. Within minutes the system had deposited its information into the depths of NECROMANCER's computer and disconnected. Suddenly another call came in, then another. As the clock on NECROMANCER's desk moved dutifully through the night a multitude of systems interacted with NECROMANCER's. The box of Marlboros emptied, followed by half of another one.

NECROMANCER considered the fact that the virus was multiplying quickly. Even the randomization algorithm which was built into it would not be enough to hold back the flood of calls in the near future.

NECROMANCER knew that soon they would have to implement phase two of ENCHANTRESS. This would effectively quadruple the telecommunications capability of the project. NECROMANCER would contact SAPPHIRE tomorrow through the dead letter drop. SAPPHIRE would then discretely route three more telephone lines from the Brooklyn main switching center. He would mark each as inoperable and note this mindfully in the telephone company's computer system. These lines would not be conspicuous, as only incoming traffic would be passing through them. Had they been used for outgoing calls, the telephone company's computers would have reacted quickly. Ma Bell did not completely trust her employees when it came to unauthorized telephone usage.

NECROMANCER's superiors had decided on using untraceable lines. Even though the calls would be made from other computer systems into NECROMANCER's computer, they had decided that untraceable lines would be safer. Better to error on the side of caution than to have such an important project compromised. Besides, the use of untraceable lines was something tangible for those involved in the project who did not understand the technical aspects of it. It gave them a sense of reassurance in doing something they understood, when everything else was as understandable as a Voodoo ritual or medical surgery.

The similarity to the ENCHANTRESS program and medicine was not just some idle simile. ENCHANTRESS was a computer virus, and very similar in its design, life, procreation and proliferation to its organic equivalent. Like an organic virus, the computer virus infected normal cells (or programs) for the express purpose of replicating itself and thus insuring its continuance.

The virus which NECROMANCER had developed was designed to monitor the communications capability of its host computer to determine if access could be made back to NECROMANCER's system. If no access was available then it would wait patiently for the trigger sequence which had been programmed into it in much the same way an organic virus may lie dormant for months or even years in its host. If the infected computer system had a communications capability then the virus would discretely inform NECROMANCER's system of the viruses location and how to access it. At the same time the virus would watch for opportunities to infect other systems, either by injecting itself upon any removable disk that touched the infected system, or via the telecommunications facilities that the infected computer possessed. Thus, much as humans catch the flu by being in close contact with people who have the flu virus, other computers caught the ENCHANTRESS virus by coming into contact with the infected computer system.

NECROMANCER's system accumulated the data on accessible systems. The accessible systems were where NECROMANCER expected to be able to show the most horrific results. Covert entry into these systems, aided by the ENCHANTRESS information opened a wealth of opportunity to NECROMANCER's superiors. However it was the home or personal computers which surprisingly made infection of the larger systems possible.

Thousands of people move data between home computers and work computers every day. Many times work computers are tied into larger computer systems via a network. It is this indirect path that NECROMANCER had anticipated and had written ENCHANTRESS to exploit.

The plan had been successful.

Since the virus had been introduced, only two months ago, it had successfully reported over 10,000 penetrations. Many of the systems were of no interest to NECROMANCER except that they provided breeding grounds from which the virus could springboard to other systems.

Like a true biological virus, ENCHANTRESS lived to recreate itself at the expense of its host. Every system that touched an infected system was doomed.

The infection was spreading at an exponential rate. Soon there would be no systems left to infect. That was when ENCHANTRESS would make itself known to the world.

NECROMANCER was exhausted. It was the exhaustion which followed unadulterated exhilaration. The agent disconnected the system, turned off the lamp then removed the ashtray and headed for the door. It was time to sleep and to dream of things to come.

May 1, 08:21 EDT

Jahmal and Evan were in his office working diligently on the latest Iraqi data. Evan got up and moved toward his computer system to work on a related task. Some references had been made to a Russian computer system and Evan wanted to check and see if there was a reported penetration on that system.

Jahmal looked up as Evan headed toward the computer system. "You scored pretty big on this Iraqi chemical plant stuff."

"As a matter of fact some of the credit belongs to you. Seems that list of hobbies that you gave me for the engineers over there gave me the key to one of the guy's passwords," replied Evan.

"Really? Well that was their mistake. Once the great Evan Smith got in they didn't have a chance, I imagine."

"They'll never know I hit 'em. It was an old PDP 11/44 running RSX. It's easy not to leave footprints in a system like that."

"What really concerns me is some interdepartmental mail I got a hold of. I can only make out the chemical equations but with chemical weapons being so hot I thought that I'd get you in here first thing to sort through it."

"Well I can translate it Evan, but I won't be much good at evaluating it from a technical aspect. Who do you have doing that? ," asked Jahmal.

"Gary Eagleton is down the hall. He was read on a couple of weeks ago. You remember him from the Afghan project, don't you?"

"Oh yes, I remember him," replied Jahmal. "Very talented."

"Yes he is. The capture of that antidote formula was a real coup. The Mujahedin were really getting hit hard with that biological weapon until we found the antidote. As soon as you get the basic translation done you can take it down to him. The printouts are right here," said Evan as he handed the small man a stack of computer paper. "I've got a lead on another break that I'm going to work on for a bit."

"Okay. You want me to put the genius at work sign up?," joked Jahmal.

"No, that's okay. They'll smell my keyboard smoking and know," Evan shot back.

Jahmal left to his office to work on the translation of the document as Evan moved to what appeared to be a technological shrine on the other side of his office. He reached down and pressed a master switch that brought the mass of technology to life.

Evan loosened his tie and removed his jacket as he sat down to the computer. The equipment interface to a variety of communications equipment that rivaled anything else in the world.

From his sanctuary, Evan could reach out and attempt to breach virtually any computer system that was connected to the world, no matter what the medium. He had access to satellite equipment, telephone systems, fiber optic systems, all from the safety of his discreet fourth floor office.

Evan realized that the communications equipment was a boon but also a real threat to security. To reach out and touch the target computer Evan had to expose his system and his attempts to the scrutiny of whoever might happen upon his communications.

When he was not attempting to infiltrate targets his communications gear was physically disconnected from the computer. Having infiltrated systems for years, Evan was not about to trust any permanent link of his system to the "world."

Evan connected the telephone line to the modem and entered in a series of commands which instantly put him in touch with an information system in France. In a matter of minutes he was connected to a target computer in Moscow through a surreptitious trail that made him look like a Cuban intelligence officer.

The system was not of much interest, it was sucked dry on a weekly basis by one of the junior computer operators on the third floor. What did interest Evan was the progress of a virus which he had inserted onto the host computer. The virus was designed to give him information about access to other computer systems.

As he entered the system, he typed a series of commands which awakened the virus. He activated the download portion of the program from his end and watched intently as the computer burst compressed data back to his computer in Maryland.

The process took only seconds thanks to the compression algorithm which he had written into the virus. As soon as he was done he put the virus back into its monitor mode and retreated, making sure to reset any evidence of his ingress into the computer. He did not wish the Cuban intelligence officer to notice that his login had been used.

Evan quickly disconnected the communications equipment and activated the evaluation program to decompress the data which he had recovered.

Immediately, he noticed that the data did not look normal. Evan moved closer to the screen and stared at the data. There, appended to the data he expected, he found the unusual message "ENCHANTMENT complete... awaiting instructions."

May 3, 00:27 EDT

NECROMANCER had dutifully sent the communication to SAPPHIRE requesting implementation of phase two. NECROMANCER arrived home from work, donned coveralls and proceeded to connect the new communications lines into the hidden den. The phones were hooked into a rotary so that the virus infected computers only needed to know one telephone number. Even that number was only an access number into a wide area communications network used by many "subscriber" information services throughout the country to allow local access for their users.

Having connected the phone lines to the communications equipment, NECROMANCER insured that the house was secure and then retreated into the den to watch the night's activities.

The rapidity and number of connections staggered NECROMANCER's mind. Never had NECROMANCER imagined that the program would be as virulent as it was proving to be.

Based on the number of incoming calls, NECROMANCER knew that as many as four systems were not able to communicate with the computer for every one system that could and for every computer which was able to get through on the phone another five would get busy signals.

With these calculations in mind NECROMANCER composed an encrypted message for SAPPHIRE apprising him of the anticipated saturation date. The agent smiled as the last digits of the date were encrypted. Sooner than expected, NECROMANCER's plan would be known to the world.

May 3, 6:30 EDT

Evan was puzzled by the peculiar message that he had found the other day. At first he thought that the virus had been discovered and that he needed to destroy it before it could be dissected.

Upon closer scrutiny of the data however, he noticed that the message appeared in several places in the data.

Each time the message was preceded by a login to a computer system. Evan's virus was designed to record logon identifications, passwords, and the announcement text to the system. This enabled him to infiltrate other computers, virtually at will. He had dismissed the data as some program that was running on the computer he had infiltrated and had put it on the back burner while he finished gathering the data on the Iraqi chemical plant.

Now that he had time to analyze the data more thoroughly, the pattern that Evan saw was evident. His virus was picking up portions of another program's output string. It was the computer equivalent of crossed wires.

Evan resolved to further examine the virus to remove this mess-up. He also decided to check with the analyst on the third floor to find out about the program that had given the bizarre message.

He picked up the phone and dialed Dave Anderson, the analyst on the third floor who was in charge of the CYCLOPS project.

Evan didn't know where they got the awful cover names that were used for the various projects. It was rumored that there was a little old lady who had been in

33

the intelligence agency long before computers and that she was responsible for assigning these names. When a project became defunct, the little old lady would file the word away, never to be used again.

"Dave, this is Evan do you have a listing of programs for CYCLOPS?," asked Evan over the secure phone sitting adjacent to his terminal.

"Just a second," replied Dave, flattered to be noticed by Evan. "I'll pull it up."

Dave jumped from the session he was working on and pulled up the listing of all the programs resident on the CYCLOPS computer. These lists were compiled regularly, to monitor the target's programming capability and uses. CYCLOPS was a low level administrative computer. It was used to store personnel data.

"Yes, here it is," Dave continued. "What do you need?"

"Do you have a piece of code that contains the text string ENCHANT or any derivative of the word in it?," Evan queried.

David pulled up the search utility and entered the string phonetically, The program would find anything in the listing which contained the string ENCHANT or any variations of it. Within seconds the computer flashed a negative response.

"No, I don't," Dave replied. "There isn't anything with ENCHANT either in the source code or in the compiled programs. The last time we checked was three months ago though."

"Listen," continued Evan. "Run a MIRROR on the CYCLOPS. If anyone asks, tell them that it is priority alpha and that we have a possible compromise."

"Okay," sighed Dave, thinking of the intense effort involved.

MIRROR was another virus. It was designed to literally copy the entire contents of a system back to the sanctuary in Maryland. The effort was intense because the data had to be compressed in much the same way that Evan's program did. It then transmitted the data piece by piece back to the secure systems. There the data was decompressed and used to create a virtual double of the target computer.

The effort was painstaking and the tension was always high when MIRROR was performed. Usually MIRROR was run when the system was being backed up by the target's system operator. The intense effort was hidden by the backup procedure. To run MIRROR outside of the backup schedule meant that the data had to be in even smaller pieces, and that a multitude of sessions would have to be used and reused. Each entry in the computer logs had to be meticulously removed as well.

"One of my viruses tripped up some output from a program with the word ENCHANTMENT in it. It might be nothing but I want a damage assessment for Paul by tomorrow AM. Which means I need your MIRROR two hours ago. Sorry pal," said Evan.

Evan hung up the phone and stared pensively at the wall before him. He was extrapolating the possibilities like any good programmer. Studying every aspect of the presented problem, trying to determine the best plan of attack,

Breaking from his trance, Evan turned to his computer with the quiet fervor that pervaded everything he did. Evan pulled up the virus code and started to examine its operation. It had been put into place over a year ago in several different machines. The program was designed to watch inter-computer connections and establish how those connections were made.

Evan pulled up the most recent download from CYCLOPS and compared the output with the portions of the program which put the data into the download file. Somehow the output had been changed.

"It's almost as if the virus caught a virus," Evan thought to himself. "Looks like all that time playing core wars might pay off."

Core wars were a favorite pastime of Evan. It was a computerized version of the Roman coliseum. Several programmers wrote small programs which were simultaneously loaded into a computer system's "core memory." Each program tried desperately to alter memory, asserting its position, and hopefully destroying the other programs which were attempting to do the same thing. The victor was the program which remained intact after all the others were destroyed.

Evan had rarely been beaten when he played. Of course he played with some of the most ingenious programmers in the western intelligence world. This restriction had been placed upon him from the outset. It was decided that if some of Evan's core war programs fell into the wrong hands that the damage to national security could be irreparable.

However, this situation was no game. If his virus had indeed been infected, then it could be exposed at any time. Within the next twenty four hours he would have to isolate this ENCHANTMENT program and know it even more intimately than the original programmer. "After all," thought Evan, "the best defense is a good offense."

Dave stood and rotated his head in slow stretching circle.

It had been seventeen hours since the MIRROR had been requested and he had just watched the last of the data burst into one of the several computers designed to receive it.

He moved across the room and logged onto the Cray supercomputer. Normally he would not have had priority on this system but the priority Alpha declared by Evan had changed all of that.

"Maybe this is the big break I've been waiting for," Dave thought hopefully to himself.

He longed to work under Evan's tutelage up on the fourth floor.

A high school graduate, who had exploited several large scale computer system on the West Coast, Dave had been recruited by COMPOPS before his identity could be released to the press. In exchange for his "enlistment" COMPOPS had pulled a few strings and made the entire incident disappear.

COMPOPS' mentors were willing to bend the rules to acquire the most ingenious people in the industry. Once inside the COMPOPS organization, though, strict adherence to the rules was required.

The rules weren't tough to follow. In fact they made a lot of sense even to Dave. The rules of the job paled in comparison to the benefits of working in the ultra-modern facilities of COMPOPS. Dave longed to excel in the organization and viewed Evan as a master craftsman who could help him move up in both his technical abilities and in his position in the organization.

Dave loaded the QWIKGLUE program on the Cray. This program was designed to decompress the hundreds of megabytes of data from the computer and recreate the system on a designated target machine much faster than regular GLUE program which David was usually relegated to using. Still the job would take another three hours.

Dave shrugged the sleep from his head and headed for the cafeteria. He needed a heavy dose of caffeine and something to quell the growling which was building in his stomach. He had learned from experience that he should eat light when pulling these all-nighters. Too much heavy food and he knew that his body would be begging for sleep. It was better that his body crave food for a little longer in order that it forget about sleep.

As Dave headed down the hall he noticed a few other lights on. The job demanded a hell of a lot from its people. Fortunately the COMPOPS personnel were fervent about their work.

It seemed to Dave that each time he worked on a project, whether routine or not, time slipped by unnoticed. It was as if the computer terminal mesmerized its true followers, singing its own siren song.

Dave rounded the corner and headed into the cafeteria.

One of the many benefits of working for COMPOPS was that the cafeteria was inexpensive and open twenty four hours a day.

It was hard enough for the COMPOPS personnel to survive on their government paychecks in the Washington area, and the rural location of the facility made it hard to find anything more nutritious than a Big Mac, or a Subway sandwich within ten minutes of the facility.

Dave grabbed some cold cereal and supplemented it with some fruit, He then selected the largest Styrofoam cup and filled it to the brim with steaming black coffee. As he moved toward the dining tables he noticed Paul and Evan sitting in the corner.

Evan noticed Dave and motioned for him to sit with them.

"Hey Dave," Evan called out, as Dave moved within earshot. "How's it going?"

"I just started QWIKGLUE," replied Dave as he set his tray down across from Evan. "Should be three hours, max."

"Good. Paul and I were just talking. I'd like you to help me once we have the system loaded. I know that you've been doing some advanced studies in computer virus detection and you know CYCLOPS like the back of your hand."

Dave fought to restrain his pleasure at this suggestion. This was the break he had been hoping for.

"Great!," Dave replied. "Do you think you could have tripped up a virus on the other side?"

"I don't know yet. Could be, but we'll have to wait for the GLUE to dry so we can look at CYCLOPS in detail. I've already sent the self-destruct code to SEEKER though, so we only have 48 hours to assess the damage or we'll have to abort the CYCLOPS program."

"Man," said Dave. "If the self-destruct takes effect how long for you to mutate the virus?"

"Only a few days," returned Evan. "I know how much that project means to DIA. But it's better to play it safe than risk a major compromise."

"I'm going to try and catch up on some paperwork before people start to show up. This is the only time of the day that I can get it done," said Paul as he rose from his chair.

"Okay," sighed Dave. "I'm going to finish this and then take a light nap. I'll give you a call in a couple of hours. I've been here all night watching the MIRROR. Real exciting if you know what I mean."

"Great," replied Evan as he rose from his chair and grabbed his tray, "We'll see you in a bit."

Dave turned to his meal and tried to finish it. He knew that he wouldn't be able to sleep but he had to try. The excitement of working on a major project was giving his body a rush of adrenaline. All Dave could hope for was that the GLUE would dry quickly so that he could get work on the project.

Dave had worked rigorously to make the grade since coming to COMPOPS. He had worked toward getting his BS in Computer Science from George Washington University with the help of government education funding, He hoped someday to be allowed to go to MIT to do doctoral studies in computer security. He showed a great deal of self-motivation in his work for COMPOPS and felt a sincere debt of gratitude to the organization and to Paul Sanders in particular for his help in keeping Dave out of serious trouble with the FBI.

Like the other government employees, he felt a deep sense of satisfaction in his work and showed a great deal of dedication to the organization for which he worked.

The sense of satisfaction helped somewhat to offset his meager government paycheck.

Dave finished his breakfast, thinking of the possible career growth that could come if he worked well with Evan on this new project. "Maybe even get an office on the fourth floor," he thought to himself as he got up and headed back to his office.

May 4, 8:22 EDT

Dave awoke to the quiet chirping emanating from his terminal. It was the Cray alerting him to the fact that the GLUE was complete. He had been working intently on another project while he waited for the QWIKGLUE operation to finish, but fatigue had cornered him and put him down for the count. Dave acknowledged the alert and picked up the secure phone to call Evan.

"Evan," started Dave, "the GLUE just dried. You ready to dissect this thing?"

"Yeah, Dave," replied Evan. "Listen, I want you to make sure that everything that this code has touched is sanitized. Call the hardware jocks and give them the same priority I gave you earlier. Also make sure that the target machine is completely isolated. I want one terminal hooked up to it and no more than ten feet of cable between the machine and that terminal."

"What's up?," questioned Dave, surprised at the extreme measures which Evan was insisting on. The sanitization was standard, but the other measures seemed rather extreme.

"I just found this same situation on a computer halfway across the globe," shot back Evan. "This thing must be extremely virulent. Until we find out exactly what is going on I want to treat this as a possible internal infection. I've already called Paul. I'll meet you in the clean room in 10 minutes."

Dave swiveled around and started typing furiously at his terminal. He flashed the hook on the phone and called the hardware team to insure that every piece of equipment used for the MIRROR and the GLUE was sanitized immediately. He then called the install team and made sure that Evan's instructions were carried out explicitly.

Having done all of that, he secured his terminal and made for the clean room where the target machine would be waiting.

As he traversed the halls he pondered what little he knew of the problem. Evan had not had time to brief him on the project yet. But from what Dave could ascertain two distinctly different computers from two different target countries had been infected with what seemed to be a virus. Somehow that virus had made itself visible to Evan's SEEKER program.

The SEEKER program was famous within COMPOPS. Every COMPOPS analyst was required to undergo training in the basic tools used by the agency and SEEKER was the cornerstone of the entire COMPOPS operation.

Until Evan had developed SEEKER, breaking into the target computer systems had been the point of greatest risk. For projects that couldn't be exposed using SEEKER, this was still the case.

However, with the implementation of SEEKER, infiltration into entire networks of computers within hours was possible. This was because SEEKER existed solely to monitor the infected computer for excursions to other computer systems. It then transported itself across the network onto the next machine and repeated the process.

Every infected machine carried the route information to the first infected machine. In this way any information obtained by the viruses as they progressed were passed back to the original infiltration point. As this route information was accumulated the infiltration point virus communicated the progress of the virus throughout the entire network.

Somehow the SEEKER program had discovered a program which had infiltrated at least two different systems with virtually no connecting points. The thought frightened Dave. The ramifications were obvious. If SEEKER was compromised then a different methodology would have to be used to break networks. This could set the agency back years in its efforts to monitor foreign countries' classified information.

Dave rounded the corner and saw Evan and Paul standing in front of the clean room. As he approached the two they turned and looked at him. Neither had the usual carefree, almost cocky expressions that they usually wore. In fact they both looked as though the world were about to end. "If we don't solve this problem then our world just might end," thought Dave to himself.

"What's up?," queried Dave.

"Paul ordered a scan of the last years traffic to see if this was more than a coincidence. It seems that within the last two months there has been an exponential increase in the number of computers with the words 'ENCHANTMENT COMPLETE' on them," replied Evan.

"My God!," gasped Dave. "How many references are we talking about?"

"Over 10,000 targets," answered Paul.

"Let's see if we can beat this thing then," returned Dave.

"Before it beats us," he thought to himself.

Evan grimaced and turned to open the cipher-locked door. Suddenly Dave realized the weight which these men whom he admired had to carry every day of their lives. It awed and frightened him. It also allured him to aspire to their levels of expertise. "Simply no accounting for taste," he thought to himself.

As the door opened and the three entered the clean room the task before them was made even more awesome to Dave. The clean room was a barren, operating room like environment. There was a single terminal hooked up to the computer and a single power cord extending from the machine into the floor. The stainless steel tables and stark furniture reinforced the impending sense of gloom, even death, which Dave had felt when he had entered.

The terminal which was attached to the computer was a sophisticated piece of engineering. If a dumb terminal were on one end of the scale then this one represented a superman terminal. It was capable of performing a variety of tasks independently of its host. It was even able to capture the operating instructions of the computer and analyze them before they were allowed to perform on the host. Tracing, encryption, deciphering, and debugging were all standard capabilities of the terminal. It also had the ability to simultaneously display the values of data in several different regions in the computer's memory in any given numeric base that the operator desired.

Both the terminal and the host were conspicuously marked with the bright red biological hazard symbol, along with a bright yellow lightning bolt. This was COMPOPS means of marking machines designated for destruction because of exposure to virulent computer programs.

"Let it not be said that COMPOPS did not have, at the very least, a twisted sense of humor," Dave thought to himself.

Evan switched on the terminal while Dave prepared to boot the host machine. He only did so when Evan indicated that he was ready to monitor every aspect of the computer's awakening. The entire "boot" sequence would be recorded and then compared against the known boot sequence from the previous MIRROR on the machine.

Evan stared intently at the terminal and nodded gravely at Dave. Dave turned on the computer and started the boot sequence. As the machine came to life, Dave moved beside Evan and watched the values of the machine's internal registers changing on the terminal. He knew this machine intimately, but he trusted the analysis program on the terminal to a much higher degree. Any deviance would cause the terminal to stop the host so that the operators could analyze the deviance before proceeding.

The boot sequence completed normally and Evan logged onto the machine in one of the many sessions displayed on the terminal. Evan and Dave watched as the login proceeded. Evan ascertained that the SEEKER virus was in place and functioning normally. He then opened a window to the virus so that he could watch its operation.

"Evan," Dave said, "on my way down here I was thinking about this and it came to me that this might be a program similar to SEEKER. That would account for the appearance of the erroneous data in SEEKER's data buffers."

47

"Yeah," said Evan, a smile coming to his lips. "Great minds do think alike."

"I was thinking the same thing but I was going to run the host through all the paces before I pursued it because I didn't feel comfortable about starting there unless someone else had the same idea. Think we should set up a communications link?"

"Sure," replied Dave, excited to think that Evan and he were on the same wavelength. "If I were you I'd route the link back to the WORM system on the terminal so that it can't get hold of the machine."

The Write Once Read Many (WORM) disk system is an optical storage system that allows data to be stored on a laser disk. Because of the technology used, the data can only be written once, unlike other computer storage systems which actually "write over" data once it is changed. The super terminal WORM system was designed to prevent errant programs, or viruses, from destroying or modifying the operating system or OS, the set of instructions that allows a computer to function.

Evan smiled, and started typing furiously at the keyboard. He set up the required configuration and then returned to his session on the host computer. He typed in the command to remotely connect to the remote system he had just created on the terminal. Suddenly the terminal began to alarm in several different windows. As Dave and Evan looked at the alarmed windows the magnitude of their discovery hit them both.

Paul broke the silence. "What's going on guys, you've only been working on this for fifteen minutes. Has it got you stumped already?"

Dave and Evan turned and smiled to each other. Then Evan turned to Paul

"You are not going to believe this."

"I think that someone has created a self-mutating communications exploiting virus and secreted it upon at least 50,000 foreign computer systems."

It seemed to Dave that Paul turned white. He looked at Paul and then at Evan. The concern on his face was easily discernible. "Are you telling me that someone else has created a SEEKER like program?"

"That sums it up pretty well boss," Evan replied. "The scary part is that according to the systems that we detected this infection in, that this puppy could have hit the U .S. at least 30 to 60 days ago, depending upon where the original penetration occurred."

"Do we have any idea who is behind it?," Paul asked.

Evan looked at Dave and they both turned and looked at Paul. "We've only been working on this thing for about 15 minutes Paul. Snap out of it," chided Evan jokingly. "Maybe if we had the documentation, we might know."

Paul half-grinned. He looked at Dave. "Didn't I warn you about using unauthorized copies of software?"

Dave was totally baffled. He appreciated Evan's and Paul's sense of nonchalance in the face of what he thought was a catastrophic nightmare. "Sorry boss," he replied. "I just wanted to play Pacman, they didn't tell me there was anything else on the disk."

Paul smiled, glad to see that they had taken some of the edge off of what was definitely not a joking matter. "You two get back in there and start digging. I guess I 'll go call the big guys and let them know that we've got a definite problem."

"This is all they need," Evan said. "First a damn land war and now a techno war to boot. Sounds like pure misery to me."

"Well, just hope that this is some dumb hacker who accidentally had a bright idea. If this thing is a serious threat by some country or terrorist group, we're in deep doo-doo," Paul quipped. "I'm headed up to the war room. I'll call you guys later to see if there is anything else you have learned, or need."

Paul turned from the other two and headed for his office. As he turned the corner, he prayed that this was just the creation of a good hacker. The other possibilities were just too frightening to contemplate.

Since COMPOPS' inception, part of their charter had been to watch for any sign of a counter-virus activity on the part of other nations. As far as COMPOPS knew, computer espionage to the degree that it was practiced by COMPOPS was the equivalent of the atomic bomb before the Soviets had developed their own. It was COMPOPS' job to insure that the advantage was maintained.

As far as Paul knew, there was no evidence of success by any other country in creating a self-mutating SEEKER type program. This new development did not bode well for COMPOPS' monitoring activity if this ENCHANTMENT virus truly had been developed by a foreign government. SEEKER and other methods had been utilized to forestall the development of such programs by other countries. If this was a concerted attempt by a government then Paul would have a lot of explaining to do to the powers that be.

The first thing that Paul needed to do was alert those powers about what had been discovered thus far.

He entered his office and unlocked the box containing the direct line to the White House. It was fifteen minutes after nine in the morning on May fourth. Duly noting the time in his log, he picked up the receiver. "This is Paul

Sanders, Project Omega, I need to talk to the President immediately. This is a priority Delta Foxtrot 3 message."

May 15, 00:25 EDT

NECROMANCER had watched the progress of ENCHANTRESS for the last two evenings. An urgent message informed all involved that phase three would be ready to commence on the 15th of May. With the movement into phase three NECROMANCER had to disappear along with the computer equipment. That morning a telephone truck had appeared at the end of the block and removed any tell-tale wires from the terminal block.

NECROMANCER packed the necessary gear into two impact resistant aluminum cases and prepared the incendiary devices, NECROMANCER then opened the window in the back bedroom and moved quietly down the fire escape to the alley. Someone struck a match to light a cigarette in a van parked at the end of the alley.

This was the "all clear" for the agent.

NECROMANCER moved quickly and confidently toward the van.

The agent entered the van, closed the door and handed a remote detonator to one of the occupants.

The dark complected man looked down at the detonator and threw the switch.

At 20 minutes past twelve the townhouse blew apart in what the fire department would conclude was a natural gas explosion. Nothing was left of the infrastructure of the house. Unfortunately the building on the other side had also been destroyed. Its occupants mutilated beyond recognition.

At fifty minutes past midnight the entire area surrounding the townhouse was put under the control of a team of special investigators for the FBI. Three of its best agents had been killed in what was considered a routine investigation of a possible terrorist sympathizer. If agent Eugene Randall had anything to say about it there was going to be hell to pay.

Eugene Randall, G to his coworkers, was a towering aging black FBI agent. He had cut his teeth on cases during the 1960's, helping to infiltrate the more violent black supremacy groups. He hadn't felt as though he was betraying his race. He was an advocate of the teachings of the Reverend Martin Luther King Jr., although to admit this during those times would have surely meant dismissal from the Bureau. Violent militarism tended only to detract from his race and its just cause, in Agent Randall's mind, and he was glad to have played a role in quenching such harmful influences.

Randall arrived at the scene at about five minutes to one and immediately checked in with the units responsible for securing the area. It seemed to him that there was just too much coincidence in the fact that a target of surveillance had been blown up along with the team that was doing the surveillance.

One of Randall's teams had been set up in the adjoining house because it had been ascertained that the person under surveillance had been heavily involved with computer systems. This team had been responsible for acquiring data from the suspect's computer system through electromagnetic radiation (EMR).

Eugene Randall didn't particularly like the operation, or understand the technology involved. He was the operational coordinator, responsible for making sure that the technical surveillance as well as the physical surveillance were coordinated and staffed and that no one blew the operation.

Eugene Randall took it very personally that the EMR surveillance team had been blown up. The second team, the physical surveillance team, had been stationed across the street where they could gather the requisite photographs and material evidence. At the sound of the explosion, they had called in to the Bureau and notified them of the tragedy.

Randall had been in bed when the call had come in. He had dressed quietly kissed his wife, as he had become accustomed to doing when departing in the middle of the night, and had sped over to the scene.

Fortunately there had been little destruction due to fire in the FBI house. The three agents had been killed because the support wall between the two houses had been collapsed and caused the upper floors of the building to collapse.

As soon as the bodies had been removed and the situation brought under control, a recovery team went into the FBI house and extracted what remained of the computer surveillance equipment. These systems were ruggedized in a fashion similar to the data flight recorders in airplanes and had suffered the building collapse much better than their human operators. The machines were ruggedized not in anticipation of this kind of incident, but because there was a limited amount of this kind of equipment available to the FBI and it traveled constantly to wherever it was needed next.

Randall let the NYPD arson and forensics teams get started on the laborious job of collecting physical evidence from what was left of the suspect's house. He made sure that he knew who was responsible for the investigation on the local police side, so that he could obtain any information if the need arose.

Agent Randall checked to make sure that all these tasks were started. He then checked with his physical surveillance coordinator, Mike Zvaboda.

"What happened Mike?", Randall started.

Zvaboda maintained his professionalism despite the fact that three of his coworkers had just been crushed to death. The towering young man was of Russian stock, which was clearly evident in his full face and dark hair and eyes.

"I still don't know, G," Zvoboda answered. "We were sitting there snapping pictures, and the EMR team told us that there was none of the usual activity. We figured it was going to be a slow night. The suspect had cut off all the lights and it looked like we could take it easy, and then Boom! The whole building went up. We called emergency services and to Bureau and then tried looking for survivors, but we couldn't get through the debris."

"It's okay Mike," Randall reassured the young agent. "This could be just a fluke. You guys did the best you could. You didn't see anything unusual before the explosion?"

"Nothing out of the ordinary," Zvaboda responded. "It was just normal front building kind of coverage, trying to figure out if the suspect was up to any unusual activity. You can check the logs for vehicle movements and that kind of stuff, but I sure didn't see anything that would make me think that something like this might happen."

Randall let the young man go.

He liked Mike and was sorry that something like this would happen on his shift. At the same time he was glad that Mike had been in charge. He was cool-headed and knew how to handle most situations. There was no telling how some of the other agents might have responded to this kind of situation.

Randall knew that Mike had done everything by the book and that if there was an answer to find, Zvaboda's professional response had preserved that answer for the finding.

May 16, 20:30 EDT

Within two hours of Paul Sanders' original call to the President a crisis center had been established in COMPOPS. This center was manned only by COMPOPS personnel. However, Paul had been sent to be a liaison in the crisis center at the White House, which had been set up thirty minutes after Paul's first call to the President.

Evan and Dave had worked ceaselessly to try and dissect the virus into its major components. The code was robust, and had to be meticulously "disassembled."

They had accomplished quite a bit since they had first detected the virus, eleven days ago. They were running on pure adrenaline, working 12 and 15 hour days in the small clean room, trying to dissect the virus that they had discovered. They had found mutations of the virus on several different types of computers, in several parts of the world. They were carefully dissecting the code to discover its purpose and the means of its mutation.

The phone outside of the clean room began to ring and Dave stepped out to answer it. Dave came back in. "Evan it's Paul. He wants to talk to you."

Evan left Dave to continue the disassembly and walked outside to the phone.

Evan liked the kid. Evan was the kind of person who could quickly and precisely evaluate a person's capabilities. He had to rely on his instincts about new people because of the many times he had been forced to work with them.

This was a world of "response teams" and "crisis teams," teams of every kind, individuals thrown together by fate and the fact that they possessed the capabilities to respond to the demands of a specific job. In Evan's book, Dave had passed the ring of fire and he considered him as a very valuable and efficient tool, one that Evan needed desperately in this situation.

"Yeah Paul?"

"Evan, do you think that Dave can continue on the project alone?"

"Why?," Evan replied. "You getting ready to can me?"

"I'm serious, Evan," Paul continued. "I have an urgent matter that only you can resolve. Do you think the kid can handle this by himself, or should I take time out to bring one of my other Alpha team members up to speed?"

"As far as I'm concerned this kid should be one of your Alpha team members. Why have you been hiding him downstairs?"

"It's a long story. I'll tell you it sometime. You just confirmed what I felt from the beginning. Get your ass down to the White House. The chopper is on the roof."

"Yessir," joked Evan. "Need me to bring you a fresh change of underwear?"

"You're not coming down here to see me, you're coming down to see the President," Paul answered more seriously.

Evan said good-bye and hung up the phone. As he headed toward the helipad on the roof he wondered what he had stumbled onto and why the hell he was headed to see the President when he should be home in bed.

May 16, 21:00 EDT

Evan hated flying.

Helicopters were the worse. It seemed that they rattled constantly until it seemed the shaking would never leave his bones. As he transited between COMPOPS and the White House he occupied himself with thought of the virus he and Dave had started to dissect. He felt confident that the President wanted a technical evaluation of the virus and knew that he could not bog down the dissertation with a lot of computer talk.

What Evan had already discerned about the virus was startling. Whoever had developed it was well grounded in computers, that was obvious. It seemed that the program had a translation module which allowed it to mutate and adapt to its host's environment. In layman's terms this meant that the virus could ascertain which computer it was on and then "rewrite" itself to accommodate that computer. It was unique in this sense. Evan had made the SEEKER self-modifying but he had never thought of the method employed by the author of this ENCHANTMENT virus.

The virus also seemed to be capable of considerable damage. That was what Dave was back at COMPOPS trying to dissect at this moment.

The damage assessment and the trigger were currently the two main modules which needed to be identified. These modules were the equivalent of the detonator and the dynamite in a bomb. Only instead of destroying material this bomb destroyed information, information which was the key to any "advanced" society.

If Evan and Dave failed in isolating the trigger and the damage modules there was no way of preventing this virus from being used to extort the owners of infected systems.

There were already cases in the annals of computer crime which showed that many large corporations were willing to pay extortion money rather than allow the public to learn of the vulnerability of their computer systems. Some major computer corporations were even suspected of deliberately putting "holes" in their programs and defects in their hardware to insure repeat business by the buying companies.

The helicopter started to hover and then gently descended onto the White House lawn. Evan thanked the pilot over the roar of the engines and then stepped out of the craft, stooping and half running to escape the wrath of the loathsome beast which had dropped him here in the middle of the night.

As he approached the entrance he was greeted by Paul and a Secret Service agent. The agent rapidly searched Evan and then allowed both Paul and Evan to enter.

"Sorry you had to fly," apologized Paul, who knew of Evan's intense hatred of that mode of transportation, "the old man wanted to see you ASAP."

"Besides," quipped Evan, "you need to use that helipad or they'll turn it into an exercise area."

"Seriously," Paul continued, "I want you to listen to the old man and take careful consideration of what he has to say. Whatever you decide, you know that I'll support you 100 percent."

"Why do I have this distinct feeling that this isn't going to be a pleasure visit?," responded Evan.

At that juncture, Paul and Evan reached the crisis center. An armed Marine guard logged Evan in and gave him a badge which identified him as part of the crisis team.

Having completed the formalities, Paul ushered Evan into the crisis center itself.

Evan noticed some familiar faces from FBI and CIA as well as from some other agencies which were "no-such." As Evan scanned the room he noticed the President, sitting at the head of the table. He was dressed casually and as always had a fatherly, compassionate air about him.

As the President noticed Paul and Evan's arrival he excused the rest of the members of the team and asked them to return in an hour. Evan sensed an ominous task was about to be laid before his feet, and he didn't like not knowing what that task might be. He only knew that if he were here merely to brief the President that the other members would have remained to hear his briefing. With their departure Evan felt totally exposed.

"Mr. Smith," the President said as the door closed behind the last man, "can I call you Evan?"

"Of course, Mr. President," responded Evan.

"Evan, Paul here tells me that you are probably one of the foremost computer experts in the United States, maybe even the world. He has also apprised me of the situation we have with this damn virus, and the fact that your program was the reason that we spotted it at all."

"I don't know what to say Mr. President," replied Evan looking somewhat embarrassed by the praise from such a high source.

"Well, you don't have to say anything, Evan," continued the President. "When a man does as much for his country as you have there isn't much that any man can say, even myself, to make you feel any better than you do just knowing what you have accomplished. However, we need to discuss what might be done now to help our country. That is why I have called you here at this God awful time of night."

"Uh-oh," thought Evan, "here it comes."

"Paul here tells me that there is really no way to know where this damn virus has spread or who may have planted it. Damn, he says you don't even really know what this thing is designed to do. The only thing that he says you do know is that some program that you've written is the only method of quickly determining where this thing exists."

Evan was a quick study and knew where the President was leading. He couldn't believe that the President, or Paul would even suggest what he knew logically was coming.

"What we'd like to know Evan, is how quickly can you modify your program and infect the key domestic computers."

"What we had in mind," Paul jumped in, "was a hunter virus. Something that would expire within a given amount of time and do nothing more than let us know who is infected and maybe kill the virus program if you can figure out the destruct mechanism in time."

"What about the COMPOPS charter?," asked Evan, incredulously. "We've been prohibited from executing those kinds of operations, and frankly I agree with the policy. Stealing foreign secrets is one thing, but..."

"Evan, we simply want you to come up with the contingency. You're the only person who can rapidly develop a discreet program that we know that we can trust not to have any back doors. We have some other leads that we are working on, but honestly they may not pan out. We need you on this one."

"With the Middle East still in turmoil, we are at an increased state of vulnerability. I wouldn't put anything past that maniac Saddam or his followers. We have decided to proceed with this operation as if it were a significant threat to both national and military security. Until we know what this thing does, and who wrote it, it will remain that way."

Evan weighed the possibilities in his mind. The memory of Lt. Colonel Oliver North's betrayal by superiors with good intentions was still a current event. The man had taken physical risk to himself and to his family and had been left to the jackals when the plan had fallen apart. Good intentions had been the seed for many of history's most devastating failures and humanity's most oppressive devices.

Still, Evan knew that if he did not acquiesce that some second rate programmer might be put in charge of the project and that Evan would have no means of controlling what seemed to be a much desired course of action.

Evan was not being vain.

He simply desired to make sure that this project didn't exceed its bounds. He also appreciated the President's feelings about this being a strategic military threat. The Iraqis had been paying for the education of a new generation of Arab with the goal of achieving technological parity with the West. This could be an Iraqi threat.

"What kind of control will I have over this project?," asked Evan.

"Total," answered Paul. "You design the code, infect the systems, and insure that the virus self-destructs upon your command."

"Of course the presidential finding will be taken care of," said Evan as he looked towards the President.

"Actually," the President responded, "it already has been taken care of, Evan. Paul thought that you were a good team player and would be amenable to this course of action so I had the finding drawn up earlier. I'd like you to read it before I sign it."

Evan reached for the documents the President offered him. He sat down and scrutinized the material. It justified limited actions which were specifically outlined in the interest of national security. The actions outlined did not exceed the bounds of what Evan thought was reasonable.

Evan looked up at the other two. "I'm exhausted. Can I get a couple of hours of sleep before I get started on this?," he asked half joking.

"Son you sleep as long as you like. I need you at your absolute sharpest," replied the President.

"Before I crash Paul, I'll give you a list of what I'll need," said Evan.

"Fine," replied Paul. "I've got a room booked for you a couple of blocks from here. You can drive there in about 10 minutes."

"Great," answered Evan, he was about ready to collapse as the fatigue engulfed him.

May 17, 10:30 EDT

Evan had slept fitfully.

Upon awakening he had made arrangements to return to COMPOPS via a safer means of transportation, had showered, and then headed down to the hotel restaurant. It was eleven o'clock and Evan expected a hassle for trying to order breakfast at such a late hour, but the staff was used to such requests and he received his order quickly.

He ate slowly and read the paper. He tried to give his mind time to itself without the hassle of worrying about the project ahead of him.

A few minutes after finishing his second cup of coffee, a COMPOPS driver appeared, ready to take Evan back to the COMPOPS offices. Evan rose, left a tip and charged the meal to his room. As he and the driver headed toward the exit they exchanged idle conversation about the Oriole's winning streak and about the soon to be heavy summer traffic to Maryland's Eastern shore, a favorite get-away of many local residents.

They got into a beige government issue sedan and headed up the Gladys Noon Spellman Parkway, better known as Interstate 295, towards the COMPOPS complex.

Suddenly the secure phone began to ring.

The driver answered and then passed the phone to Evan.

"Evan, this is Paul," came the voice at the other end. "I just wanted to check on where you were and how long it will take you to get to the office. I wanted to tell you that we have everything on your shopping list and that we are ready and waiting on you."

"Okay, Paul, I'd say we'll be there in about 50 minutes," replied Evan. "How is Dave doing?"

"He's coming along almost as well as you would," joked Paul. "He's nailed down the trigger and is working on it now. It's damnedably complex from what I gather; multiple accesses, multiple encryptions, that sort of thing."

"Okay, Paul," replied Evan. "We'll be there in a bit."

Evan hung up the phone and returned to his paper. Time passed quickly. The traffic was light compared to the morning and evening rushes that caused cars to crawl up the thirty some miles between Washington D.C. and Baltimore.

Except for the few privileged individuals who could afford to live in the elite neighborhoods and those few crazy individuals who dared live in the less protected areas, practically no government employees lived in D.C. proper. D.C. had been surrendered to working poor and to the indigent.

It shocked Evan that the nation's capital could be such a monument to the failures of capitalism. The area surrounding the White House was a virtual combat zone for gangs and drug dealers. As a result the swarming mass of humanity required to keep the federal government functioning commuted, some extensively.

The driver pulled off of 295 and within a matter of minutes they were entering the underground garage designated for the small COMPOPS motor fleet.

Evan exited the car and said his farewells to the driver. He immediately headed for the direct access elevator and made his way to the fourth floor to check on Dave's progress.

Evan exited the elevator and headed immediately for the clean room. He entered the access code on the cipher lock and waited for the familiar click of the bolt retreating. The door opened and Evan entered. There sat Dave thoroughly enthralled in his work. Evan noted that they had moved a cot into the room and that the room was cluttered with what looked like the remnants of breakfast.

"Kid, you give a whole new meaning to the words clean room," joked Evan.

"Did you get any sleep?"

"Yeah, a couple of hours," replied Dave. "Sorry about the mess but I started tracking this second trigger and didn't want to take time out right now."

"Don't worry about it," came Evan's reply. "If the trash gets too high, we'll just break out the scuba gear."

"How's it coming?"

"Well most of the text is encrypted. The instructions are pretty straight forward. I even stumbled over the mutation code which allows it to move itself to other machines. The triggers are tied into that code very tightly. It mutates the destruction sequences on not only the type of computer but on some sort of algorithm which determines the computer's primary functionality."

"You said that you were working on the second trigger?," queried Evan.

"Yeah," replied Dave. "The first was really straight forward. It was completely Intel 80x86 level code to reformat all the storage devices it could. It has a hard coded counter that checks how many times the routine has been called and then fries everything."

"Not much you can do about that one," answered Evan, "Except keep the counter level below the trigger level. What's the one that you are working on now?"

"This one looks tough," sighed Dave, the hours of exhaustive work showing in his voice. "I've isolated the code to IBM SYSTEM 37 assembly language. A great deal of the trigger strings look encrypted. I found the offset to what I think is the destruct sequence but it looks like that is all encrypted as well."

"Have you thought about finding the decryption algorithm?," asked Evan.

"This guy is slick," answered Dave. "The encryption is one way. He takes the strings that he is looking for and passes them through the one way algorithm and then does the comparison. The only thing that I can say for sure is that whatever system this is geared for won't see massive data destruction. This guy has something in mind for whatever type of IBM system he is looking for, and it isn't random destruction."

"Listen," said Evan, "instead of trying to break all of these damn triggers one at a time, just identify the subroutine areas, the type of computer it is geared for and hopefully the offset to the destruction modules. I'll try to get some super spook help on the decryption algorithm. Deal?"

"You got it boss," returned Dave, relieved for the direction in what seemed like a never ending jigsaw puzzle.

"You think maybe we can get some more help in here?"

"It's already on the way," smiled Evan. "By this evening you'll have a full staff including a couple of Alpha team pros."

"Great, do you still have something that I can do?," asked Dave, who was relieved to see more help but disappointed at the thought of returning to the third floor.

"I don't know," Evan answered solemnly. "If you would be willing to be my deputy and run this project on your own, I guess I could fit you in."

Dave stared at Evan incredulously. He couldn't believe what he had just heard.

"Do you mean that?," he asked Evan. "It's not nice to play with the souls of young outcast programmers struggling on government pay."

"I mean it," said Evan. "You've done a great deal of the work already and I need someone who thinks like me to be here when I can't be around."

"Have you cleared this through channels?," queried Dave nervously, unable to believe that something so fantastic could happen.

"Paul and I talked this morning. Suffice to say that I'm with Paul on this one."

"If Paul trusts you then that's all the more reason to for me to trust my instincts about you," said Evan, as he turned to leave the room. "Just don't let Paul or me down, okay?"

"You got it boss," replied Dave, as he returned to his terminal, recharged by the exhilaration spawned by the news Evan had given him.

Evan left the clean room and headed toward the elevators. He entered one and placed his access card in the authorization slot. The elevator panel came to life and Evan pressed five.

He waited as the computer in the elevator alerted the security personnel on the fifth floor and they verified that Evan was expected. The elevator doors closed and Evan ascended to a secret world nestled within the one to which he was already accustomed. As the doors opened he began to focus on the monumental task which lay ahead of him.

The fifth floor of the main COMPOPS building was reserved for "special projects," a euphemism which resided on the same level as "wet operations."

When there wasn't a special operation in progress, the fifth floor was used as a grand meeting room. It was used to entertain the infrequent visitors who nurtured the COMPOPS organization in what were referred to as "dog and pony" shows. Within hours the fifth floor could morph into a pulsing nerve center which had seen the resolution of numerous "Critical Situations."

To Evan's knowledge the fifth floor had never seen the likes of the type of operation which he was about to undertake. Of course Evan might not have known about every operation which had taken place on the fifth floor, but such an operation required very specialized expertise and Evan was the best in the business.

Evan greeted the guard at the elevator doors and passed into the common area. The floor was buzzing with activity. Activity which Paul had instigated at Evan's request before Evan had retired for the evening.

A series of offices had been created using partitions in the front section of the office. Toward the back of the was a computer and communications system which was beyond state-of-the-art.

Evan personally knew every individual on the floor. He had worked with each of them on previous occasions. Each individual was considered one of the foremost experts in their field. Each was also able to work quickly and precisely in the high stress environment produced by the many situations which came up in the intelligence business.

Unlike the intelligentsia of the academic world, each of these individuals was firmly grounded in reality. They all understood that the most precious commodity in this business was time.

Evan said hello to Mary, his appointed secretary in these situations. He had a great disdain for such formalities in his regular work environment, but Mary was a second pair of hands, eyes and ears which helped him in these time critical matters.

"Looks like we're stuck with each other again," said Evan.

"Yeah," replied Mary, "and I was really getting used to eight to five work."

"Give me about an hour to put together some material. I'll have the originals for you then. I'll need them put together in a briefing package for everyone forty five minutes after that. Have the staff ready for the briefing in two hours even, okay?"

"You've got it boss," replied Mary. "Any exceptions to the do not disturb order?"

Evan paused for a moment, contemplating the awesome task in front of him.

"No," came his curt reply.

Mary nodded her acknowledgment and immediately started to notify the staff members of the impending briefing. "Be there in an hour and fifty five minutes from now," Evan heard her say as he entered his office and closed the door.

Evan smiled as he hung his jacket on his chair and booted his computer system. Once Mary had her orders he knew that he would not be disturbed and that this small secret world would be in perfect order when he reemerged into it.

Evan worked diligently to put together the briefing material and assignments for his team of programmers and technicians. He had to be sure that every team had adequate requirements to work from, while maintaining a great deal of "missing information" so that no one could try to surmise the goal of the project, or its extent.

This task was made especially difficult because of the nature of software development. In a usual environment it was best that everyone clearly understood what the goal of the project was, so that everyone could utilize their talents to their fullest. There was a slight chance in a project of this magnitude, that the work assigned to each team might be considered trivial, because it typically called for programming without a great deal of creativity. If there was one thing that any programmer valued above all else, it was creativity.

Fortunately, the team that Evan had assembled was used to this kind of effort, and realized that the entire mission was no more important than the tasks assigned to them. They also respected the way that Evan developed his task structure so that as much creativity as possible could be injected into the project.

Evan soon had the briefing material ready using the Macintosh computer that he preferred for presentation work over other systems. Because the system was designed for people who didn't really need to interact with the computers operating system, the methods of manipulating and interchanging data were quick and intuitive. Because the machine was graphical in nature the development of superb presentations was accommodated very quickly.

Using the "Mac" also allowed him to give the data to Mary, who was not very computer literate, for the final touches and actual presentation creation. She loved the Mac and didn't even regard it as a computer but as a superb aid to her daily tasks.

Evan gave the data to Mary to finish and returned to his office. As he stared out his window looking toward the lush Maryland foliage, he prayed for the wisdom and determination to guide the project, and the courage to stand up to anyone who suggested that the bounds of this project be expanded, whoever they might be.

May 21, 02:00 MDT

NECROMANCER's new base of operations was located in an isolated area of New Mexico. The base was entirely self-sufficient and was equipped with some of the most sophisticated communications equipment in the world. Primary among this equipment was the satellite communications equipment. With this equipment NECROMANCER could keep in constant touch with the infected systems and command them at will, while making it virtually impossible to locate the remote position.

The satellite communications equipment was also useful for sending demands to the world, as well as for monitoring the progress of the meeting of those demands.

NECROMANCER's program had allowed access to every computer required and more. With the information provided, the agent was free to roam through the hallowed halls of secure systems without fear of censure or detection. Now it was time to start making demands.

NECROMANCER turned on the terminal connected to the minicomputer which had replaced the smaller microcomputer in New York. The message to be conveyed had been carefully written and encrypted months ago. There was no room for error at this point. If the demands were not clear and concise the officials relegated to meeting them would plead for more time, or would say that they did not understand them.

Every detail had been specified in the note, everything was feasible. Most of all, the demands were sure to be met because of the weapon which stood behind them.

NECROMANCER called up the communications program and selected the message numbered 001. The agent paused only for a second, reveling in the culmination of years of work, then pressed the transmit key. At that moment NECROMANCER could have sworn that the world had shuddered.

May 21, 14:50 EDT

Agent Randall sat behind his desk reading the surveillance reports of all the agents involved in the CREIGHTON case. Beside those surveillance reports were the autopsies of the three FBI agents and of the corpse found in the terrorist sympathizer's townhouse. Randall smelled a fish but he couldn't figure out where all the information pointed.

He was not convinced that the explosion had been an accident, although the corpse had been found in what seemed to be a secret den amongst the debris of some low level intelligence documents.

The physical description of what was left of the corpse roughly matched that of the suspect, but Randall had not come to be a senior agent in the FBI by simply concurring with the facts. His gut instinct told him that something serious was afoot and he had lost three friends in the maelstrom.

He went back over the activity reports looking for the slight clue which would allow him to peel back the layers of deception, much as a safe cracker peels a safe. He made a note to himself about several different vehicles in the area and resolved to have them followed up immediately.

As Randall sat analyzing the data before him Mike Zvoboda walked into his office.

Randall looked up.

"Hey Mike what's up?"

Mike, who was usually affable, had a look of consternation on his face.

"Something BIG has just come down G," Mike responded dourly. "The chief wants everyone in the briefing room in ten minutes."

"Any clue as to what it is?," asked Randall.

"Not the slightest. I know that the helipad has been cleared for some high level Washington brass, though," replied Mike as he turned to exit the room and notify his other coworkers.

All Randall could think of was that he probably wouldn't be able to solicit any help for the CREIGHTON investigation. "Hell," he thought to himself, "it won't be the first time you cracked a case on your off time."

Agent Randall tidied his desk and started to move toward the briefing room to see if he could ascertain the nature of the crisis. Unfortunately nobody had the slightest clue as to the nature of the situation. Randall found that disturbing in itself. Gossip was the mainstay of the office, lack of it did not bode well.

Randall sat toward the front of the briefing room and joked with his fellow agents until the chief entered. Quickly, a hush fell over the well-disciplined FBI agents. Curiosity was a common denominator among these professionals and their curiosity had been more than piqued. Each agent was hungry for the information which would lead them on the chase.

John F. Campbell was the New York Bureau chief. New York was a key assignment reserved for administrators who were being groomed for the top most slots in the bureau. "Jack" was a well-liked, no-nonsense administrator. He was known for his fairness, candor and brevity. As he approached the platform Randall thought he noticed a slight slip in the bosses usually flawless demeanor. Randall didn't know what was up, but he knew that it must be something formidable to shake the confidence of a man of Jack Campbell's character.

"Gentlemen," started Campbell, "I have called you here to brief you on a situation which has come to our attention within the last two hours. This situation is unprecedented in the annals of FBI history. Unfortunately, it is more than likely a harbinger of a new era."

"Two hours ago I received a call from the Chairman of the New York Stock Exchange. He asked me to come to his office to discuss a matter of the utmost urgency. Upon my arrival I was given an opportunity to view a piece of electronic mail sent to the chairman. This mail, although electronic was nothing more than an extortion threat. Something which everyone of us has had, or will have, the opportunity to deal with in the course of our careers at the Bureau."

At this point Jack paused to add import to what he was about to say. "While we were reviewing this note, irrefutable proof of the power of the extortionists was given to the Chairman and myself. At precisely 1350 hours all electronic transfers on the New York Stock Exchange ceased. Exactly seven minutes later transaction capabilities returned."

"The perpetrators of this extortion literally have their hands around the throat of this nation's most important financial institution."

At this point no one in the room seemed to breathe. The magnitude of this crime shocked every agent in the room.

"The story that was leaked to the press was that a failure of the main computers resulted in the loss of the data, and that the NYSE has insurance with Lloyd's to cover exactly this kind of situation. That is the story that sticks, regardless of what other claims may surface."

Jack looked up and smiled slightly, trying desperately to reassure his agents. He removed his glasses and took a drink from the glass on the podium. "Now comes the bad news," Randall thought to himself.

"If this were a simple matter of extortion, it would obviously not warrant the special attention it is receiving," Jack continued. "However, this is not a simple matter of extortion. It is an act of computer sabotage which has been instigated by agents unknown. The perpetrators have effectively infected the entire NYSE to such a degree that recovery would debilitate trading for a considerable period of time."

"We have been given until 9:00 AM tomorrow to free several terrorists who have been imprisoned and to transfer $250 million dollars to several bank accounts throughout the world. If the terrorist demands are not met by 9:00 AM tomorrow, the NYSE will be shutdown for an indefinite period of time, and the reasons will be made public."

"My chief of staff and I will be allocating assignments to each of you depending upon your current workload. Any crime which does not involve the potential loss of human life, will be considered secondary to this case."

"I also want those of you who are currently working the terrorist beat to shake your files and cross check any possible activity to try and isolate the organization, or organizations which are capable of pulling off this caper."

"Pick up a copy of the briefing material on your way out."

"One last note," Jack added, "there is a crack team coming from D.C. . They are cleared for all of our material, but not vice versa. I expect you to give them your utmost cooperation in this matter."

Randall rose and made his way to the exit where he picked up a briefing packet. He was encouraged that he was still going to be able to shake the tree on his current case. He glanced through the material as he headed down the corridor. As he entered his office he thought he came to the list of terrorists to be released. He knew that he recognized one of the names and immediately went to his files.

Many of the younger agents relied on computer systems to store and manipulate their information. Randall had never been able to feel comfortable with using a machine to store something so valuable.

He rapidly located the small 3x5 card containing the name of the person whom he had remembered. On the card were cross reference numbers of various files. He then went to his file cabinet and proceeded to extract the various files. As he moved toward the end of the list he found that one file had already been removed. He muttered to himself under his breath, thinking that he had loaned the file out to some colleague who might be able to scoop him on some small piece of information relevant to such a monumental case.

Randall returned to his desk and checked another 3x5 card file which described the contents of each numbered file. He quickly found the information about the referenced file. As he read he smiled to himself and rapidly searched through the CREIGHTON files for the one referenced on the previous card. He pulled up the dossier of the supposed dead terrorist. Toward the back was a list of known associates, among them was Jamil Qaafar, one of the seven men to be freed.

Randall picked up the phone and called Jack Campbell's secretary. "Pat, this is G. Tell the boss that I have what I believe to be a very significant lead I'll be down in five minutes." Randall hung up the phone, grabbed all of the files on his desk and made for the bureau chief's office. "Sometimes things could go very, right, even when they are very wrong," he thought.

He moved quickly to the chief's office and was greeted by Pat Allison, Jack's secretary.

"G, Jack said to let you right in."

"Thanks Pat," Randall replied.

Pat pressed a button notifying Jack Campbell of agent Randall's arrival.

Randall proceeded through the door into the bureau chief 's office. Jack rose and smiled at Randall. "Have a seat G. I knew I could count on your help, but your alacrity has left even me a little flabbergasted."

"Well, Jack, it just so happens that I think that there is a tie-in to the CREIGHTON case. If I'm right then I think we might have someone already inside the organization."

Jack seemed somewhat taken aback by the last statement. "Have a seat G. Tell me more."

"Well," G continued, "it started when we noticed the formation of a new radical offshoot of the PLO. The organization was well covered. It came to our attention because of a Palestinian student in the U.S. who decided that the dream of a homeland was never realizable. He decided to change his loyalty to a home land which could be real."

"The U.S.?," asked Jack.

"On the money," answered Randall.

"He told us of this organization which comprised mostly younger, well-educated Palestinians. We encouraged this student, ALABASTER is his codename, to continue his relationship with these students and to infiltrate their infrastructure. We thoroughly debriefed him over a course of two months and then set up a means of re-contacting him if required. We have minimized contact with him to avoid suspicion."

"This is all very interesting G, but what does it have to do with the NYSE case?"

"We started to surveil the members of the organization which ALABASTER had identified. One of the terrorists had a brother who was in the Fayhadeen. That brother is one of the terrorists to be released."

"And you think there might be a tie-in?," Jack asked.

"All the other terrorists are well known and central figures in the terrorist world. This Jamil Qaafar is relatively low level stuff compared to the rest. There doesn't seem to be any reason to put him in the same league as these other guys. My guess is that this guy's release means that this new organization is tied in."

"You think that this Jamil Qaafar's brother is somewhere in the middle of this NYSE caper?," Jack asked.

"It's not Qaafar's brother, it's his sister, and yes I definitely believe that she has something to do with this case."

"His sister?," Jack queried. "Well do we know where she's at? Send a team to pick her up."

"Well according to the NYPD we already have her," replied Randall.

"Great," Jack said as he started to pick up the phone. "Who do I call to get her released into our custody?"

"The city morgue," answered Randall.

Jack removed his hand from the phone and looked at Randall incredulously.

"G, what's going on here?"

"That's what I want to know."

"You know that we lost Adams, Mcullough and Aldershot on the surveillance gig. I think that there might be more to all of this than we have been led to believe, Give me three men and I'll find the answers for you as quickly as I can."

"I'll give you six of my best field agents," returned Jack Campbell. "Give me an answer more quickly than even you can G. This one is really important."

"Whatever you say boss."

May 21, 15:00 EDT

Evan had been working laboriously on the hunter-seeker program for the last four days. He lived, breathed and slept the project. He was sitting at his desk reviewing the project's progress when the phone rang. Fortunately, much of the work he and Dave had accomplished, was the ground work for the hunter-seeker's logic.

"Evan, this is Paul," came the voice at the other end. "I have Dave on the other line, hang on and I'll bring him in on this."

Evan heard an audible beep denoting the presence of another party in the call.

"Hey Dave, How is it going?," he queried.

"We've made a lot of progress Evan," replied Dave. "We have all of the modules isolated and have broken down all of its functionality. The only problem is ascertaining the key sequences. We still haven't figured out what the damn thing is looking for or what it will do to the various systems that it has targeted."

"I might be able to shed some light on the first system," interjected Paul. "I just got a call from Jack Campbell, the New York FBI chief. It seems that somebody has just made an extortion demand against the New York Stock Exchange."

"What does that have to do with this?," Evan and Dave both asked simultaneously.

"It seems that the computer system is the method of attack. From everything that Jack described, I think that this might be a manifestation of the virus that we have been trying to fight."

"How long was the attack?," asked Dave.

"They shut down the system for seven minutes. They gave the NYSE until 9:00 AM before they shut the system down for good and make their actions public."
"I'll do a cross check on the times involved and see if I get a correlation to module wait times in the virus," said Dave.

"Leave that to one of your staff Dave," returned Paul. "I want you both to give me a list of the tools you need, to pack your bags, and to be ready to leave for New York in an hour. Dave can you get started, I need to talk to Evan for just a minute more?"

"O.K. Paul," answered Dave. "See you guys on the helipad."

The double beep denoting that Dave had indeed hung up the phone was the cue to continue his conversation with Evan.

"Evan, I want to know how far you've come on your project."

"We've got a prototype which eliminates any signs of the virus from the test bed. The problem is that every time we run it the virus jumps in and obliterates everything it can when we delete certain modules out of sequence. It seems to be able to even physically damage the machine in certain cases. We have to work on the sequencing. Dave's work should be able to give us better insight on the last few modules."

"Can we use this thing for the NYSE problem?," asked Paul.

"I don't think we're ready yet," answered Evan. "If something goes wrong we could potentially bring down trading for quiet some period of time. If it were the weekend then I would say risk it, but with it being Monday we would never be able to minimize the damages."

"Okay, Evan. Do you think that the project will continue on if you go up to New York?"

"Yes," answered Evan. "I think it would be beneficial to go up there and see this thing in person. Everyone has their assignments and I won't be gone that long."

"You know that this means you'll have to get on the big bird," chided Paul.

"A man's gotta do what a man's gotta do," laughed Evan.

May 21, 17:00 EDT

Evan had taken a Dramamine before the flight and was thankful that he had. The weather had been somewhat turbulent thanks to the onset of a cold front. He bided his time by reading a dissertation by the eminent Dr. Fred Cohen.

Cohen had been one of the foremost chroniclers of virus technology. The world at large dismissed his early warnings, but several very astute people in the intelligence arena not only listened to Fred Cohen, but extrapolated on his ideas and methodologies.

The helicopter finally landed.

Evan, Paul, and Dave were greeted by the FBI Bureau chief and led from the roof directly to computer nerve center for the NYSE. The entire area had been cleared discreetly. Evan and Dave had the entire computer center to themselves.

"Paul, I'm going to need the SD terminals set up here and the printer and disk drives set up along that wall," Evan called out as he quickly surveyed the layout of the room. "Make sure that all the external communications are cut off. If anyone hassles us what is the cover?"

"We thought that a PBX failure should cover any telephone access queries. There are a lot of T1 and satellite communication links though," answered Paul.

"Instead of a PBX failure let's make it a failure of the communications routing computer. Something along the lines of a double disk failure. We'll say that they lost both the master and the shadow machine because of a power surge," said Evan, his cat-like instincts kicking in.

"You got it," replied Paul. "Do you want to meet the MIS director while we get set up?"

"Yeah, that would be great," came Evan's reply. "Dave you make sure those guys get the stuff set up ASAP. Call me when we're ready"

"You got it boss," answered Dave.

Paul and Evan exited the computer room and made their way past several officious looking individuals guarding the entrance to the complex. They had been very thorough in evaluating Evan's, Paul's and Dave's credentials before giving them access to the computer room.

"FBI?," Evan asked Paul as they walked to the MIS director's office.

"Something like that," Paul replied. "Can't really go into it. They have orders not to mess with us but God help the cleaning lady or anyone else who isn't cleared."

Evan took the comment at face value. He never cared for the physical portion of this business. As far as he was concerned, his job simply was a matter of national self-defense. As long as the bad guys knew that we knew what they were up to then everything stayed peaceful. Evan didn't know if teaching interrogation techniques to organizations such as the SABAKH was in the same league, or the same universe for that matter. Nevertheless, Evan had to deal with those kind of people more than once in his career. It always left a bad taste in his mouth all the same.

They approached the MIS director's office and entered. Evan surveyed the room as Paul made the introductions. The office was that of a very self-assured computer professional. The walls were adorned with various awards which highlighted a distinguished career. As he faced the man who supposedly owned the office, Evan was taken aback.

"Glad to meet you Mr. Smith," said the man as he extended his hand toward Evan. "Richard Dempler."

The man whose hand Evan shook was pale. An ashtray on his desk was almost full. It was obvious that within a period of a few short hours this man had been presented with a horrible apparition which could effectively break him for life.

"I want you to know that we're here to try and keep this thing from affecting operations. Any ideas you can give me would be of great help. As Paul mentioned, we have considerable resources to try to prevent any delay in trading tomorrow," Evan explained, trying to bolster this almost broken computer professional.

Dempler smiled the half-smile of a condemned man. "Well let's sit down and talk. I've got a diagram of the complete layout of the operation over here on the conference table. Would you care for anything to drink?"

"A cup of coffee would be great," answered Evan.

"Nothing for me Richard," replied Paul. "I've got to go over and talk to Jack Campbell. I'll leave you in Evan's capable hands."

Evan smiled and walked toward the conference table as Paul exited. "Let's get to it Rick. Do you mind if I call you that?"

"Evan you can call me anything you like as long as you kick this thing's butt," replied Dempler, smiling more deeply now.

"Rick that's what I'm here for. I need information you can give me though. I'm here to kick this thing to hell and back but you're the guy that has the intimate knowledge of this mammoth system. You and your people have to be my eyes, ears, and my knowledge base," answered Evan, trying to help this man who he knew was critical to the success of the mission.

Dempler seemed bolstered by Evan's confidence. He moved toward the table and started to describe the huge system for Evan. As he did Evan saw the man who owned the office they were in start to return to his normal self, bolstered by the reassurance that he was getting the help of some of the best in the business.

Eugene Randall was used to leg work. Like his aversion to computers, his penchant for building intensive networks of informants was viewed as obsolete by many of his younger coworkers.

Fortunately, there still existed a few young agents who were willing to learn the true trade craft of the "G-man." Mike Zvaboda was one of these men.

As G and Zvaboda exited the car, Mike checked the area. He knew that their presence would be noted by the complex network of lookouts, who served as a first defense for the numerous crack dealers who operated in the area. G had taken precautions against being "made" as cops. They had taken Mike's beaten up Nova from the Federal building that evening, and both Mike and G wore inconspicuous clothing.

"You always catch more flies with honey. Is what my grandma taught me," is what G had told Mike.

Many of G's informants didn't know that G worked for law enforcement, let alone that he was an FBI agent.

The two agents ambled towards the coffee shop on the corner as though they had all night before them with nothing to do. Many times, an agent undercover blew it because he displayed a sense of purpose which was uncommon in the environs in which he was trying to fit into. As with any culture, fitting in meant more than wearing the native costume and speaking the local language. This was another tactic which Agent Randall had painstakingly taught Zvaboda.

The two finally entered the coffee shop after engaging in idle chatter with several "Home" boys who knew Agent Randall, or thought they did. Randall made greetings to a few more familiar faces as he and Zvaboda moved to the back of the coffee shop.

The man they had come to meet was sitting at a back table reading a racing form. Had the racing form been on the seat beside him, Randall and Zvaboda would have taken another table, had a cup of coffee or two and left. This was a warning sign that could be adapted to any prop which fit the environment and had proven invaluable for maintaining Randall's clandestine liaisons' security.

The man put down his form to greet his old friend and several minutes of idle, yet very audible chatter ensued. The two ordered coffee and pie and after its arrival the tone of the conversation proceeded to move slowly down the decibel scale, as though the newness of the meeting was wearing off.

When Randall was comfortable about the amount of time which had transpired he deftly moved to the true topic of conversation. "What you got for me from our man on the street?"

The man opposite Zvaboda and Randall answered quietly, "He said that the girl that you are looking for took an extended vacation. From what he can gather she went out west. Everything is on the QT so finding out the exact location doesn't look good."

"Did he have any suggestions for me to follow up on?," Randall asked, hoping that he might have a thread that could be pursued from the outside.

"He said that there were only radio communications to her location, microwave and satellite stuff. He also said that they had taken parkas and that kind of thing, so it is probably located in the mountains. He'll keep his ear to the ground but the tension level in his group is ultrahigh."

Randall started to raise the level of the conversation again. To Mike it was as though a conductor had skillfully moved an orchestra into a subtle pianissimo and then back. The transition was so subtle that even the most astute listener would miss the small passage which had contained the important exchange.

The retreat was as protracted as the entrance, carefully orchestrated to continue the deception. The effect was analogous to that of the magician's patter, designed to mislead the audience and subtly convince them of the reality of the performance.

Randall and Zvaboda re-entered the car and exited the area. The whole process had taken over an hour. Mike was impressed by the care which Randall exercised. He had not even seen the exchange of money which he knew had taken place.

Randall broke the silence. "Damn, looks like we're gonna have to do some inter-agency cooperation on this one. F***ing satellite communications. What's this world coming to?"

"Used to be that we'd tap some phones, which would lead to some payphones or residential phones near these suckers and then move in for the kill."

Zvaboda knew that Randall was upset. Unlike many cops, Randall rarely expressed himself in such expletives, unless he was undercover or extremely upset.

"We'll have the taps in about 20 minutes. Maybe we'll get something G. We still have about 14 hours."

"Yeah, this whole technological mess is getting to me. I hate to think that I lost three agents because of some damned computer bullshit." replied Randall.

"It happened G," answered Zvaboda. "It might be a different weapon but it's the same shit, right? I mean look at what the Thompson machine gun did, C4, hand-held rocket launchers, it's all the same. Things change."

"You're right Mike. You know me though, I already feel like a dinosaur. Damned technology is changing so quickly anymore that I don't even feel safe at home. VCR's, microwaves..."

"Indoor toilets," finished Mike, smiling.

"Damn straight," laughed Randall, "damn straight."

May 21, 20:30 EDT

Paul Sanders had ensured that the set up at the NYSE would proceed without a hitch and then went with Jack Campbell back to his office. As they entered the office Jack started to let Paul know about what had been learned about the supposed perpetrators so far.

He extensively detailed the suspected organization which Eugene Randall thought was linked to the operation and told Paul that Randall and his team were out combing the streets at that very moment.

"What are the chances that your people can find the people that wrote this virus before the payoff time," Paul asked.

"I really think it's a long shot Paul. G. Randall is one of the best field agents I have. The problem is that you see what kind of measures they took to eradicate any trace of this girl. She was probably our strongest lead to these people, although we didn't know it until now. Even if we found her we're not sure where she falls into all of this. I think that it will really be up to you guys to get the NYSE out of this one. We'll catch them, but not in eleven hours."

Paul shook his head in agreement. "Evan is the best, Jack. He's got a head start on this one but I don't know if eleven hours are going to be enough for him either. We have a contingency plan though and that's what I came here to discuss with you. The fact that you guys have some possible leads could be very beneficial."

"I agree," Jack replied. "Whatever we have that you guys might be interested in let me know."

"Which reminds me, I think we have some EMR surveillance from the townhouse this woman was staying in. If it would be of any use, I'll get you copies of the stuff."

"Why don't I have Dave look the stuff over with your EMR guys to see if it's of any value," Paul replied, trying to disguise his excitement over the possibility of a significant break, by seeming to be only professionally polite about the request.

Suddenly, Jack Campbell's intercom interrupted. "Sir, Agent Randall is here and says that he needs to talk to you urgently."

Jack looked to Paul for an okay which Paul gave him. "Send him in," Jack replied.

Randall walked in the door and closed it behind him. He hadn't changed from his undercover clothes and still look every bit the bum.

"G, this is Paul Sanders from Washington. We were just discussing the terrorist angle on this extortion deal," Jack said.

Randall nodded to Paul and then turned back to Jack. "I think we might need some inter-agency help on tracking this one boss. My contact in the organization relayed it back to me that the girl has split to some area, probably mountainous, out west. It's so remote that they are using satellite communications to the site."

Paul interrupted. "I think that we might be able to try and locate any satellite uplinks through some contacts in D.C., as soon as I can use the scrambler to get somebody working on it."

"That would be great," replied Randall. "I've got some of the other men trying to figure out what type of vehicle they used to extract her. Next shift will start on tracing some unusual activity in the area the last couple of days she was there. Zvaboda and I are about ready to pack it in if that's O.K. with you. I don't think we're going to get much farther on this before the deadline."

"That's fine G," Jack answered. "I think you've done a hell of a job considering the time frame we have to work in."

"Thanks boss," Randall said as he turned to leave the room. "We will catch these guys. I promise you that."

"I know G."

"Nice meeting you Agent Randall. I'll get someone working the satellite angle within the hour," Paul said as he watched the beleaguered Randall close the door. He then turned to Jack. "Now...about that contingency plan."

May 21, 23:48 EDT

Evan and Dave had been working on isolating the infected areas of the main trading computer system for more than five hours. They had delegated the laborious work of ascertaining the reliability of the backup data to Rick Dempler's computer personnel.

Evan hoped that they might disinfect the computer's essential program using the SD terminals to stop any damage which might be attempted because of deletion of the virus modules out of sequence. If this plan failed they would hopefully have identified "clean" backups of the critical programs.

They were working at full intensity, trying to get the massive system cleaned up before the 9:00 AM deadline was reached. Everyone realized that all their effort would be for naught if they had not entirely disinfected the system by the deadline. As Evan entered the command to delete an identified module warning screens on the SD computer began to flash.

"Shit," cursed Evan. "Make a note that deleting module 27A1 forces module 199B7 to try and destroy the system."

"Got it," replied Dave. "That makes sense, now that I look at it. Look at this Evan. I think that we may have the delete sequence."

Evan stopped his work and looked at Dave's suggested sequence for removing the code. He was thoroughly impressed by the kid's ability to follow even the most intricate threads.

"Looks like you might have it," whispered Evan. "Whaddya say we try it?"

Dave smiled weakly. He knew that one mistake in the sequence and they would have wasted time which could be spent manually deleting the code. He trusted his work though, and Evan's suggestion lead credence to the logic of what he was proposing.

"You're the boss."

Evan half-laughed, "If it doesn't work we'll just take it out of your paycheck, okay?"

The two worked for 45 minutes putting together a quick program to perform the delete sequence. The deadline drawing nearer as they typed furiously at their terminals. An hour after they had decided to act they had the program ready to run.

"Go ahead and start it Dave," urged Evan.

"What? You're the boss. I'm just the sidekick, remember?"

"Dave you came up with the sequence. I believe its going to work or I wouldn't have spent an hour putting it together. Trust your feelings, Dave, start the program."

Dave typed in the command to start the cleansing program. As he hit the execute key he winced. Dave and Evan both stared intently at the SD computers, which would stop any problem which they had not anticipated. The computer screen indicating the progress and success of the program scrolled on. In another screen the map of the infection inside of the computer system started to clear, module, by module.

As the indicators for the modules turned from red to green, indicating successful removal, Evan and Dave began to breathe normally. Within 20 minutes the operating system was sanitized and the program moved to clear the modules out of different resident programs.

At that juncture Evan turned and looked sternly at Dave. "Come on I'll buy you a cup of coffee."

Both men smiled, knowing that they had just won the battle, if not the war.

Dave and Evan left the program to run, confident that it would clear the system of the virus without further negative impact. They went to Rick Dempler's office to tell him of their success.

As they left the secure area and headed toward Rick's office they noticed a janitor at the far end of the hall. They were careful not to discuss any classified matters. As they walked by the janitor they were commenting on the recent cold front which had encompassed the eastern seaboard.

The janitor seemed preoccupied with maneuvering his cart around the two gentlemen. Neither Dave nor Paul heard the barely audible whisper of the camera's shutter as they approached the cart. The janitor was confident that he had accurately photographed the two men who seemed to be spending a great deal of effort in the computer center. It was almost time for his dinner break, and Hassan would discreetly pass the exposed film to his superior along with the information which he had obtained. These infidels would not circumvent the will of Allah.

Dave and Evan entered Rick's office. The grin on both of their faces immediately put Rick into a good mood. "You must have made some headway, you guys look like you just ate the canary."

"Well we've managed to write a program which is in the process of removing the virus. It cleared the operating system already, now it's working on your installed images and regularly run programs. Dave saw the pattern and we decided to give it a try. It's working like a champ."

"Do you think it'll clear everything by the deadline?"

Evan looked at his watch. There were still two and a half hours until the deadline. He quickly estimated the speed of the program based on how fast it had cleared the operating system. "I think that we've got it beat. You'll just have to avoid running any of the offline programs until the vaccine program has cleared them. Your main system should be functional before the deadline, though."

"If you'll excuse us, I'm going to head over to the operations center and call Paul and Jack downtown. Dave will stay here and monitor the operation. I think the danger is over Rick."

"I want to thank both of you for everything, I really don't know what I would have done if you guys hadn't come in. I've been in this business a long time and I never really considered the possibility that we could be impacted by this kind of threat."

"Paul has arranged to have a couple of security experts from D.C. to come up and keep this from happening again. He'll bring your people up to speed on some of the newer infiltration techniques. Dave, do you want to catch something to eat before I book out of here?"

"That's okay, Evan, I think I'll watch the vaccine's progress for a little while longer, at least until the base system is cleared."

"Okay give Rick a call when that point is reached, and keep his staff apprised as each of his offline programs are cleared so that they don't mess up and put this thing back in."

Evan headed toward the door and Dave turned to follow. As they headed out the corridor they passed the janitor whom they had seen earlier. He had a lunch bucket in his hand and was headed out the door. As he approached he heard Dave talking to Evan. "Sure is a good feeling boss."

"Know what you mean Dave. Don't work too hard, I'll call and check on you in a couple of hours."

Hassan made a mental note of the conversation. He was sure that his superiors would be pleased with the pictures and the information.

Dave headed back toward the computer center, while Evan headed toward the special operations van which was parked discretely near a rear entrance. He used his key card to gain access to the rear of the van. Inside things were relatively quiet. The young communications officer was reading a novel and one of the "guards" which Evan had noticed earlier was sitting back watching television.

"I need a secure line to Paul Sanders," Evan said to the communications officer.

The communications officer quickly punched a few buttons which activated a regular telephone link to FBI headquarters. Once he got Paul on the line he quickly started the scrambler system. It synchronized with the unit on Paul's end and a green light came on.

"You can use that phone," said the comms officer, pointing to a phone located on small desk.

"Thanks," said Evan, as he picked up the receiver. "Paul?"

"Yes, Evan, how are things going down there?"

"We managed to identify and code a viable vaccine algorithm. We should have the main system cleared by the time the deadline hits. I've advised Rick to keep his staff from running offline programs until we have them cleared as well. He seemed a lot happier than when we first met."

"I imagine he would be," Paul replied. "I've learned some interesting things from Jack and his staff. I've allocated resources to try and identify and isolate the communications center where the bad guys are running the show."

"You know who these guys are?"

"Jack and his staff got a lucky break from an active case that they were working on. Seems like there is a very significant tie in to female whiz kid named Jasmina Qaafar. Looks like they faked her death and then moved the operation from the Big Apple to somewhere in the west."

"Jasmina Qaafar? That name sounds familiar. Have you run her through the directory?"

"We sent her name in a few hours ago. I'm still waiting for the results. I'll let you know what turns up."

"Great, listen, I think that Dave stumbled onto something very important and I want to get back to D.C. to see if it fits into the other project I'm working on. Dave can handle it from here. Think you can get me back?"

"Sure, I'll have a car pick you up in about 30 minutes."

"Thanks Paul, I'll see ya when I see ya."

"Okay, pal, go get 'em. There is one other thing though that I thought you might be interested."

Evan's curiosity was piqued. "What's that?"

Paul smiled to himself, he and Evan had known each other for a long time. He only wished that he could be there to see Evan's face as he told Evan of the EMR surveillance of the Qaafar residence. "The FBI had

Jasmina Qaafar's apartment under EMR surveillance. They thought that we might like a copy of the logs."

Evan was almost knocked off of his feet. Unlike Eugene Randall, the significance of EMR surveillance was not lost upon Evan. Evan knew that all computer equipment emits Electromagnetic Radiation or EMR. This radiation can be easily received by a modified radio receiver and changed back into computer instructions, or text with very inexpensive equipment. Evan also knew that the FBI had some very sophisticated EMR surveillance equipment that could log and replay this data. It was used experimentally to record the transactions of large drug dealers who more and more were using computers to track their businesses. Because the EMR receiver typically is geared to capture data from the terminal (the nosiest part of the computer system) before it goes into the computer, or after the data has been retrieved and is being displayed, the need to decrypt the data is removed. In essence it is like looking over the person's back as they look at their computer screen.

"I'd like to see it, but I gotta get back," Evan replied.

"Well, we've arranged for a meeting with the EMR guys in the morning, but Dave and I can handle it if you want to go back," Paul answered, smiling at the thought of Evan's excitement to see the data.

Evan laughed aloud, "Great, why don't you send me a copy of the data, if you can swing it."

Paul laughed aloud. "Sure Evan, I'll see what I can do."

"Great, see you later."

Evan hung up the receiver and let the communications officer do his stuff. As he sat in the van waiting for his ride, he kept trying to remember where he knew the name

Jasmina Qaafar from. He was still working on it when the black limousine pulled up outside the van. "Oh well, just another piece of a very big puzzle," Evan thought to himself.

May 22, 04:30 EDT

Hassan's superior relayed his information and his photographs quickly to the operations center. He was pleased with Hassan's work but knew that the information itself did not bode well for the first mission. He conveyed his thoughts to his superiors along with facsimile transmission via the satellite uplink.

Thirty minutes later Hassan received an updated action plan and a revised time schedule. Immediately he contacted the members of his cell to try and put the plan into action. Unfortunately the target had left the scene approximately 45 minutes before the terrorists were able to get into place.

Hassan's superior immediately notified the operations center of the unexpected move and informed them that the departure did not seem to indicate a great likelihood of success for the proposed action.

Eugene Randall's informant was a member of that team. Once the team was brought off of active status the informant headed back to his flat. On his way he stopped in front of an all-night doughnut shop to tie his shoe. No one would have noticed the small green mark which he left on the sidewalk. No one that is, except for a member of agent Randall's team who had been looking for just such a mark for the last six hours.

The agent left the comfort of the stakeout van and proceeded to cross the street and enter the doughnut shop. He bought a cup of coffee and three chocolate glazed doughnuts. As he left the shop he dropped a napkin on the sidewalk and bent over to pick it up. He noted the color and orientation of the mark and headed back to the surveillance vehicle. The agent immediately picked up the cellular phone in the van and made a call.

"G, this is Bob, seems our pigeon left some droppings."

"How long ago?," Eugene Randall asked, quickly shaking the sleep from his head.

"About 15 minutes ago. It's a green diamond."

"Okay," replied Randall, "meet me in the office in 30. Call all the other members of the team and have them do the same."

"Right."

Randall came to life and moved across the room to get dressed. He moved quietly and without a light. His wife stirred but did not wake up. She had been an agent's wife for 35 years and was used to these nocturnal disappearances.

Randall moved quietly to the side of the bed as he strapped his shoulder holster on and kissed his spouse lightly on the forehead, quietly thanking her for her understanding and love all these years. He then moved out the bedroom door and down the stairs. As he exited he insured that the security system was on and that the door was locked.

As Randall headed toward the office he started to plan the extraction which the green diamond indicated. The color of the diamond noted that the informant felt that his cover was still in place and that he wished to be extracted for a short period of time to convey information which could not be conveyed any other way. Randall decided on a course of action and pulled up to a pay phone to let the informant know of the plan.

Randall dialed the telephone and cleared his throat. A sleepy quiet voice answered the phone. "Hello?"

"Ralph?," Randall asked, sounding half drunk.

"No, I'm sorry there is no one named Ralph here," came the voice at the other end.

"Whaddya mean there ain't nobody named Ralph there?," said Randall acting indignant. "Is this 555-6701?"

"No, I'm sorry this is 555-6709," came the reply.

"Sorry man, guess I dialed the wrong number."

"That' s quite alright."

Randall hung up the phone and returned to his car. The message had been conveyed. Now all he had to do was get his agents into place.

Meanwhile, Randall's informant returned to the relative warmth of his bed, trying to find a brief period of rest from the never ending turmoil of his duplicitous life.

May 22, 05:05 EDT

Evan was exhausted. He had slept somewhat on the return train from New York and on the car ride from the train station back to headquarters. Still, the dull throb in his head had barely subsided. He recognized this as his body's indication that it would not tolerate much more abuse before forcing a shutdown.

Evan had been to this point on more than one occasion in his life, and new how far he could push before his body broke. As he headed up the elevator back to the operations center, he resolved to quickly adapt the algorithm which he and Dave had refined in New York and then to rest for a few more hours on the couch in his office, while he let the simulations run on the test computer.

The elevator doors opened and Evan moved quickly into his office. The operations center was hauntingly still, as the skeleton crew of the night shift was off in the computer center working on something. Evan admired the dedication of these handpicked "hackers" and knew that there was no better team of people capable of dissecting and destroying this impending threat. He was also very cautious, though, and he knew that no one individual or group of individuals knew enough about the target virus or the killer virus that they were working on, to replicate either. Unlike the atomic bomb, this technology could easily be recreated.

"Hell you could write this stuff on a $500 computer from Radio Shack," Evan thought to himself. The last thing Evan wanted was another virus running around.

Evan moved toward his computer terminal and activated it. The amber glow of the screen came quickly. Evan typed in his login and password and then the classification of the file he was about to create. The file was classified at such a level that only four individuals in the world could access it. Evan trusted the other three implicitly. This had been one of his requirements before agreeing to Paul's and the President's wishes.

While four individuals could access the pieces of the puzzle only Evan and Paul could put the pieces together into a cohesive unit.

Evan had an implicit trust of Paul Sanders. He had known Paul for years, and knew what made him tick. Had he not, Evan would never have agreed to put the hunter virus plan into motion.

Evan began to type furiously, unleashing the thoughts he had been storing in his head since his last outpouring to the computer. As he typed, new subtleties became clear to him and added fuel to the fire. Before he knew it, three hours had transpired and he had finished the prototype. He quickly pulled up the commands to compile the newly created version of the virus and watched as the beast came to life.

When the virus was ready to be activated, he issued several commands which locked all personnel out of the test computer system, and started up a standard operating environment. Then he unleashed his beast into the unsuspecting computer to let it seek and destroy its prey. Evan said a short prayer for success, locked his terminal, and retired to the couch to rest. It seemed odd to him that the literal war going on inside of the test computer should disturb no one, and yet the effects could be as devastating as any real war, complete with bombs, bullets, and death.

May 22, 04:30 MDT

NECROMANCER had been informed by her superiors of the activity at the NYSE. She had also been informed that an attempt to capture her adversaries had been thwarted by their rapid departure from the area. As a result she had been ordered to execute alternate plan 001A. She readied the codes and waited for the verification from her superiors. At 4:28 a small window in the upper right hand corner of her screen gave her the order to proceed.

NECROMANCER typed the commands quickly into the keyboard and sent the instructions to the target computers. There would be no 12 hour notice before 001A went into effect. NECROMANCER knew that the consequences would be much more dramatic than those of the original 001 message.

"They will listen now," Jasmina thought to herself. "They have to."

May 22, 07:45 EDT

New York is a city of commuters. Given the millions of people that transit the face of the city every day, there is no way that they could be moved effectively without mass transit. Every morning the ritual loading and scurrying through the subways of this megatropolis' population gives new meaning to the words mass transit.

Few people, however, realize the degree to which this ritual is controlled by computers. The hundreds of trains used to move the masses to their jobs are controlled by "Real time" computer systems that eliminate the need for human intervention, The doors, the speeds, the brakes, the track switches, are all controlled by an intricate computer system. In fact the amount of information, and the amount of people moved could not be facilitated without this system.

Unfortunately, this intricate computer system also has a variety of other systems which talk to it. Like an individual who catches a cold from shaking hands with someone who has the rhinovirus, so a computer catches a virus from contacting other "infected" systems.

In the case of the City of New York's mass transit system, the virus was fatal.

At 07:47 EDT an operator in one of the central dispatch centers noticed that something was wrong. His monitor showed that four fully loaded subway trains were headed toward the same intersection, and were accelerating. He immediately turned to his superior to alert him of the problem.

While that operator was noticing the unusual activity of the four trains, the commuters aboard each were also noticing something. Unlike some computer generated graphics, and numbers on a screen however, the commuters' sensation was far more frightening. As the trains accelerated past normal stops, the commuters started to panic. Several had the good judgment to try and enable the emergency brake. However, the computers running the trains had been reprogrammed to accelerate when that switch was activated.

At 07:48:00 the central dispatch operator's supervisor ordered an emergency stop of the entire system. His command was relayed to all maintenance personnel who immediately dashed to the respective cutoff stations. The supervisor prayed for a confirmation that the cutoff had been effected as he watched in horror while the four commuter trains headed toward a collision course.

At 07:48:30 a horrific explosion and crash, shook the area of Times Square. The shaking and destruction caused subsidiary accidents above ground as people stopped their cars, fearing an earthquake. It would take rescue personnel more than 48 hours to clear the results of the four train wreck of all survivors and those not so fortunate.

At 07:48:45 the horrified shift supervisor heard the shutdown confirmation come across the radio. The confirmation was barely audible over the grief stricken cries and screams of the operators who were responsible for trying to avert New York's "Time Square Tragedy" (the moniker which the press pinned on the wreck, and resulting chaos and devastation.

At 07:50:00 Jack Campbell answered his office phone, unaware as of yet, of the riots and looting that had started because of the madness on the streets. "Jack Campbell," he answered.

A computer generated voice (later traced to the infected computer of a Denver-based telemarketing company) emitted the warning, "Do not try to circumvent our demands again," and hung up.

May 22, 08:05 EDT

Evan's head had just hit the couch when the phone began to ring. He had told Mary not to let anybody through, he knew that he was at a point where he could no longer function without rest. He realized as soon as the phone began to ring that something tragic must have happened. Mary would not let anyone through unless it were of great importance.

He rose wearily from the couch and moved toward the phone. "It better be important," he answered, not caring who was at the other end.

"It is," came Paul's voice from the other end. "The terrorists didn't like us messing around with their game plan. They got wind of it and sabotaged the New York subway computer system."

"My God," replied Evan. "How much time do we have before they shut it down?"

"We're not that lucky Evan," Paul answered. "Preliminary estimates are that 400 people are dead or injured below Time Square. Probably another 50 to 100 people have been injured in traffic accidents around the Square. The situation is deteriorating quickly as the traffic jams get bigger, and subway service is totally out. The governor is calling out the National Guard and has declared martial law. It is really a mess Evan."

"We've got to shut this thing down Paul," Evan whispered, the devastation materializing before his fatigued eyes.

"I've got the best people in the world working on it, Evan. We will stop it," Paul soothed.

"I just started running the prototype. I was going to get some sleep when you called, there isn't anything else I can do right now Paul. These bastards can literally do whatever they want, wherever they want. God knows how many systems they have infected. I feel totally useless."

"We all feel that way right now, Evan. You get some rest and let me known how the prototype does. I'll alert the President to the fact that we are about ready to institute plan JAGERMEISTER. "

"Let's hope it works Paul. For all of our sakes."

Evan hung up the phone and moved back to the couch. He lay in the semi darkness trying to rest. As he drifted off, thoughts of the hundreds of people trapped in speeding subway trains haunted him. Their screams tormented his dreams. He prayed to God that he would be able to stop this nightmare and drifted into blackness.

May 22, 12:45 EDT

While Evan slept, Paul Sanders received the President's authorization to start phase one of operation JAGERMEISTER. He had therefore summoned the men that he was currently facing. Each was the CEO of a major computer hardware or software manufacturer. He had summoned them there as a matter of national security. To each of these individuals that phrase evoked thoughts of horror. The Federal Government is a major purchaser of computer equipment. The Federal government also controlled who could purchase software and hardware and for what purpose it could be used.

"Gentlemen," Paul started. "I have summoned you here on a matter of the utmost importance. The Times Square Tragedy was caused because of a virus that has been introduced throughout the computer infrastructure of this country, if not the whole world."

The gentlemen around the table looked at each other in horror. Each had been aware of virus research and their proliferation throughout different computer operating systems. Most had been trivial, although some infections had gained national recognition from the media.

Never had any virus caused personal injury that anyone knew of. Each person knew what the results of a very malicious virus infection could be. Each prayed that it would happen to the other guy.

After an adequate pause, to allow this information to have its full impact, Paul continued. "At this moment we are working on a method of eradicating this virus. This information is classified and will not leave this room."

"What does this have to do with my hardware," asked one of the CEO's who had no equipment in the New York subway system.

"This virus concerns each and every one of you," replied Paul sternly. "We have reason to believe that approximately 85% of all computer systems which have access to telecommunications are currently infected."

There was a collective gasp as the enormity of the problem hit home.

"This virus has the ability to mutate to one or more computer platforms which each of your companies make. A list of the currently identified, computer systems, and operating systems which are vulnerable has been compiled."

As Paul spoke these words he motioned toward an assistant who moved among the members and gave them a thin bundle of photocopied information.

"The list that my assistant is passing out details which systems are vulnerable. This list does not leave the room. Neither does any of this information," Paul continued.

"Then what is the purpose of this meeting?," asked another of the members.

"The purpose of this meeting is to prepare you for measures which the President has dictated to counter this threat."

"Each of you is in a position to authorize the issuance of product changes, and to implement those changes rapidly. When we are ready you will be briefed as to the changes which will be required for each of your systems. These changes will be made to your installed base according to a set schedule."

Another gasp issued forth from the room. This one was one of disbelief, though.

"That's preposterous, the expense of what you are talking about would be enormous," shot one of the members.

"That would put my company out of business," replied another.

"The alternative," Paul continued, "is the seizure of any company not willing to comply, in the name of national security. We are deadly serious about this gentlemen. Peoples' lives are at stake, as we have already witnessed this morning."

"Stop and think of all the things which your machines control; finance, hospitals, railways, communications, air traffic, subways, refineries, you name it. Each one of these enterprises is being placed at risk. We are in a state of war gentlemen, and this game is for keeps."

The members stared at each other and at Paul incredulously. Each of these powerful men's worst nightmare had just come true.

"If there is nothing further, I will give you 48 hours to release complete contingency and readiness plans to the office of the Secretary of Defense. Good luck gentlemen, and may we all come out of this in one piece."

May 22, 13:00 EDT

Extracting Agent Randall's informant in the turmoil that was named the Times Square Tragedy, had been both complicated and extremely easy. Setting up the team in the ensuing turmoil had been the complicated part. Logistics for such a delicate operation were difficult in even the best of times. In the turmoil caused by the crash, they had almost been impossible. Had the extraction not been as critical to national security as it was, it probably would have been aborted.

The extraction itself had been made much easier because of the same turmoil. The informant was unable to rendezvous with his group because of the total grid lock that had ensnared the city. Riots and sporadic looting had broken out throughout the city as soon as the criminal elements had realized that the already thin blue line had been stretched beyond the point of breaking. It would be simple to explain to the young man's superiors that he had been waylaid in route because of the chaos.

The informant was extremely cautious, doubling back on his track several times to make sure there was no surveillance. He then proceeded into a department store which was designated in extraction plan number nine. He got off in the men's clothing floor and proceeded to browse for 15 minutes, insuring that no one was observing his actions.

When the salesman wearing a blue carnation approached the informant and asked if he could interest him in a leather flight jacket, the young Palestinian knew that several FBI agents had cleared his entire path and insured that there was no chance of a tail. He proceeded back down the elevator, exited the store, and immediately got into a black sedan parked outside.

Agent Randall was sitting in the back seat of the sedan, a walkie-talkie with an earphone was readily apparent. Randall had personally insured that the way was clear for the young Palestinian. As the door closed behind the young man, Randall gave instructions to the driver and support teams to move out immediately.

Not much was said during the ride to the FBI safe-house. There was no festive air of reunion only a sense of gravity as to the day's events, and a feeling of dread of things to come.

Agent Randall and his informant arrived in front of a large three story brownstone. Minutes before, Randall had called to insure that the parties arrival at the brownstone would not be observed by anyone who might have more than a casual interest in the party.

Zvaboda was waiting inside the brownstone along with a security team. As soon as Randall entered the building Mike began to speak. "G, some new information has just hit the papers. It seems that a 'new' organization, the Society for the Liberation of Palestine has claimed responsibility for the subway wreck. They've aligned themselves with Hussein in his call for Jihad against the infidels and have promised more acts of terror in reprisal for the civilian deaths in Iraq."

Agent Randall took a few moments to let the information soak in. He turned to the young Palestinian standing beside him and spoke to him gravely. "Looks like our friends have pulled out all the stops. We've got six months' worth of information to debrief, and very little time to do it."

The young Palestinian hung his head slightly. It grieved him that his proud and ancient race was constantly stigmatized by the cruel fanaticism of those who could not or would not work peacefully toward a solution of his peoples' plight.

After living in the West, he understood, the devastating effect that such fanatical "terrorism" had upon the his whole race's credibility.

It was to try and remove this stigma that he had gone to the FBI, not to betray his people, but to betray those of his race who used the name of Palestine to justify murder and thuggery, much as Randall had justified his infiltration of militant black organizations to try and regain credibility for his race.

It was this common ground that had helped Randall to win the young Palestinian over. The party moved into the living room to start a rigorous recapitulation of the Palestinian's last six months in the Society for the Liberation of Palestine.

May 23, 08:05 EDT

Mike Zvaboda and Eugene Randall had spent nearly twelve hours debriefing the Palestinian informant before they had called it a night. A transcriber had been formatting notes and an outline of the organization described by the informant. Thanks to the Macintosh computer that the transcriber was using the outlines and organizational charts were now on slides and ready for presentation.

Agent Randall was now standing in front of Jack Campbell, several division chiefs, and various representatives of the CIA and the Department of Defense, including Paul Sanders. The lights dimmed and Agent Randall started his presentation. "Gentlemen, we have been extremely fortunate in the matter of the Society for the Liberation of Palestine. We have had an informant in the organization for the last six months. However, while our informant can identify the critical elements you see on this organizational chart, it seems that the high tech elements of the organization have been run as a discrete entity."

"We have a limited amount of information about those elements. Also, it seems that the more conventional arm of the organization somehow became aware of Mr. Sanders' organization's presence at the New York Stock Exchange."

Paul Sanders raised his eyebrows at this comment. No one in the room knew what organization Paul Sanders direcyed. Everyone knew that it had something to do with

Department of Defense, but beyond that things got foggy very quickly. The fact that a terrorist organization had identified his personnel sent chills up his spine.

Randall continued, "They do not know precisely which organization the individuals work for. Currently they are under the belief that they are operatives for the CIA."

At this the CIA representative piped in, "Anything having to do with intelligence, they blame us. Doesn't anybody know that we only deal with international matters?"

Randall looked at the CIA representative waiting to make sure that he had finished his comments. "The organization has identified all three of the representatives of Mr. Sanders' organization who were present at the NYSE, including Mr. Sanders himself. It seems that they were targeted for extermination but left before the attempt could be fulfilled."

At this Paul's shivers turned into cold chills. COMPOPS was on the periphery of this kind of "intelligence" work. Of course the threat of violence was always there but it was not as real as for the real "spooks," cloak and dagger agents who expose themselves every day. Paul tried to keep his composure at the revelation that they had been targeted for assassination.

Jack Campbell, spoke up, sensing the overwhelming tension of the situation. "We think that we can do a considerable amount of damage to the conventional organization thanks to the information our informant has gathered. We also feel that the public capture of as much of this organization as possible, will help considerably in calming the public's fear of this group since the Times Square Tragedy."

He paused for a moment to allow these points to be evaluated by each of the members of the group. He looked directly toward Paul and continued, "We think that if we associate some computer equipment with the arrests, that we may play down the threat."

Randall interjected, "It's sort of a drop weapon kind of situation. Although in this case we won't try to violate these people's rights, by setting them up to look like they committed the Times Square Tragedy."

"We just think that during the arrests, that the presence of computer equipment and a lot of hesitance to discuss the ongoing investigation will take some of the heat off of all our agencies while we try and track down the rest of the organization."

Jack continued, "That's correct."

"We will coordinate our efforts with all affected agencies. We have already presented this plan to the Attorney General's office, late last night, and have received unconditional support for the project."

"This meeting is designed to disseminate as much information as possible to all agencies concerned, and to let you know that there will be a coordinated arrest of all identifiable terrorist operatives affiliated with this organization before the end of the day. As we speak, the surveillance teams are being put in place, and arrest and search warrants are being arranged."

"By the end of the day the majority of the Society for the Liberation of Palestine will be behind bars. That is the story that we will put out."

"It is up to you gentlemen and your respective organizations to insure to the utmost of your abilities that we readily identify and contain the rest of the organization before another Times Square Tragedy can occur somewhere else."

The meeting continued until almost 10:00. After that each representative broke away immediately to start the intensive search within the scope of their respective agencies' tasking, for the rest of the Society for the Liberation of Palestine.

As Paul left the room, he couldn't help but feel that he had a large bull's eye painted on him.

He wondered if that feeling would ever go away.

May 23, 10:35 EDT

Paul arranged a secure line from the FBI office in New York back to COMPOPS in Maryland. He wanted to pass any pertinent information from the briefing back to Evan as soon as possible. As he waited for the connection to be made, he decided not to inform Evan and David that they had been targeted. According to the information the FBI had, the SLP had been unable to identify where they were stationed. Paul's team had only been identified as targets of opportunity. In Paul's and the FBI's opinion, that opportunity no longer existed

Evan was finally connected to Paul after a few minutes. "Evan, listen, the FBI had a mole in this SLP organization, and it seems that they were able to identify the majority of people in the conventional side of the organization. However, the high tech group that we are fighting is still a big question mark."

Evan replied, "Listen Paul, I don't know if it means anything but when I was doing my masters work at MIT there was a very bright undergraduate named Jasmina Qaafar. The coincidence is too much. Why don't you check with the FBI and see if it is the same girl?"

Paul hesitated, thinking of the death threat. "Listen, Evan, did you know this girl at all. I mean, would she be able to identify you?"

Evan thought for a moment. "Well I did sub for a couple of weeks in one of her CompSci classes. I didn't really have a low profile back then. I wasn't in the business at the time, nor was I planning on getting into it."

Paul tried to remain calm, as he continued to tell Evan the pertinent information which had been brought up during the meeting. He informed Evan that, because the Times Square Tragedy had been directly linked to Palestinian terrorists and the Iraq war that the Department of Defense had been given limited permission to perform intelligence collection activities in the U.S. for the express purpose of finding the perpetrators. He also told Evan about the discreet display of computer equipment that would look like it had been seized in the raids to help calm the public.

"We've really got our work cut out for us Evan," Paul said, after filling Evan in on the details. "We've got to get your code out the door as quickly as possible so that we can avoid another Times Square kind of incident. If we don't get protected and something happens after we all start implying that we have all the bad guys, it could look bad for everyone."

"I know that Paul," Evan replied. "I think that the prototype is ready for field testing. As soon as it is installed, it should start reporting occurrences it has found, and start destroying virus mutations that it recognizes. I've made it self-learning so that when it discovers a mutation that it can't deal with that it will halt operations immediately, but nicely and request that the user contact the manufacturer."

"Good," Paul answered. "When can we have it ready?"

"Five days," came Evan's reply.

"Make it three. We need to get this baby out the door and in the upgrade kit. It will take us at least two days to get the code out to the distributors, and at least a week to get it distributed and installed in the majority of the computer base."

Evan sighed. "You never make things easy do you?"

Paul was too worried to laugh at this half-hearted jest. He knew that Evan was as burned out as he was, but he just couldn't find anything to laugh about. "Sorry partner, that gives the bad guys 12 days to figure out that we're on to them and that they need to do as much damage as possible or even mutate their virus."

"I know Paul, I just want this to be over so that we can get back to our regular jobs. This is a tough one partner."

"Don't worry Evan I have the best in the business working for me and they are doing everything they can. If we can't do it nobody can."

"But people are dying Paul. It's frustrating to feel that you could stop it."

"I know Evan. Listen, give me a call later at the New York operations center and let me know when you'll be ready. I need you and your teams in one piece, so don't burn yourself out."

Paul closed the secure circuit and headed out of the communications center toward Jack Campbell's office. When he arrived he quickly entered.

Jack Campbell looked up from his desk as Paul entered. It did not surprise him that Paul would walk in unannounced. Protocol had gone out the door and been replaced by swift and efficient professionalism. Besides, Jack owed Paul and his group a rather large debt of gratitude for their work on the NYSE problem. There was no estimating the amount of damage that would have been incurred had the exchange been shut down.

"What is it Paul ?," Jack asked.

"Jack, I think we may have a problem and I need Randall and his team to check out the history of this Jasmina Qaafar."

"Sure, is there something you need in particular ?," Jack asked as he started to page Agent Randall.

"I need to know where this girl went to school," was Paul's answer. "I think that Evan Smith may still be a target of opportunity because of his previous exposure to her. We've got to find out, and now. If we lose Evan Smith, we may never beat these guys."

May 23, 8:00 MDT

"Jasmina," the dark haired cell leader, Ibn, called as he popped his head into the operational heart of the New Mexico site.

"Yes," she replied, annoyed at the interruption of her work.

She was preparing a list of new possible targets to be relayed back to the PLO liaison and was excited by the potential of some of the new systems which had fallen under the spell of ENCHANTRESS.

"Jasmina, we have a fax transmission from New York. It is a photograph of the three people who thwarted plan 001. We thought maybe you could identify one of these individuals. Maybe from trade magazines or technical journals," Ibn continued. As he looked upon Jasmina's face he was struck by her beauty. Her dedication to the movement made her all the more desirable to him.

Jasmina's interest was piqued. She was curious to see the people who had so quickly disabled the NYSE trap. She had spent months working on it and could not imagine anyone being able to dissect and disable the bomb in less than 12 hours.

She rose and took the fax from the cell leader. She had barely taken it when she recognized the handsome sandy haired man. She could not believe her eyes. It was Evan Smith, from her MIT days.

She thought of how enamored she had been with him. His technical prowess had been the topic of conversation around the campus among the undergraduates and she had been fortunate enough to have him sub in one of her computer science classes.

She had barely been able to pay attention to the lessons, as she admired his strong build and fresh features. She had not only been enamored with his physical features, but with his complete mastery of computer science.

She had always wondered why she hadn't heard of Evan in the computer industry. Now, suddenly she had a feeling about what he had been doing all these years.

"I know this one," Jasmina said, pointing to Evan. "His name is Evan Smith, he was a graduate student at MIT when I was an undergraduate. Maybe you can check around and see where he went from there. If I remember correctly he was originally from Montana."

"We'll check on him. The New York cell seems to think that these three work for some government agency. They had very sophisticated equipment and a secure communications van."

"That would make sense," Jasmina replied. "Evan was very bright. Someone of his caliber would be well publicized by now if he had stayed in the commercial sector."

"We'll see if we can find him. How is the new target list coming?"

"Very well, actually. I think that operational plan 002 is ready but several new targets of opportunity have made themselves known as well."

Ibn acknowledged his enthusiasm and then made straight for the communications facility. He sent off a quick message to the New York cell apprising them that the sandy haired man in the picture had been identified as

Evan Smith, who had done graduate work at MIT, and to pursue the leads from there.

The message was received in the New York cell and immediately decrypted. The cell leader there, Ibrahim, called his best field operative into his office.

"Farouk I need you to go to Cambridge and see if you can track this individual down," Ibrahim said, as he pointed to the picture or Evan. "His name and the years of attendance at MIT are on the back. You are to locate and eliminate him as quickly as possible. Your tickets and car arrangements will be waiting at the airport along with means for contacting other cells which may be able to help you. May Allah be with you."

May 23, 12:00 EDT

Mike Zvaboda and two other agents were sitting atop an abandoned building directly across the street from the SLP New York cell headquarters. As he contemplated another six hours of sitting on a hot tar roof, he noticed the operative named Farouk leaving the cell headquarters. He immediately photographed the operative and noted his time of departure. Maybe their friend at the safe house would be able to shed some light on this guy's purpose in the SLP.

Unfortunately, Mike didn't have enough manpower to tail Farouk. The Times Square Tragedy had had a dramatic effect upon the city. Emergency services had been stretched to the limit, and some areas of the city including Times Square, Harlem, and sections of the Bronx had been put under martial law.

Farouk left the warehouse unaware that he was being watched. He hailed a cab at the end of the block. During his drive he could see occasional glimpses of smoke and fire rising out of the Bronx.

He was extremely proud of the blow the SLP had struck upon this loathsome American city. The Americans had been oblivious to the plight of the Palestinians for far too long. Better that they taste death and destruction that the Palestinian people had known for so long.

When he arrived at the airport an air of near mayhem prevailed. Many people were trying to leave New York until some semblance of order was restored. It struck

Farouk that a few more blows upon the huge American city could cause waves of refugees that rivaled even the Palestinian exoduses. He had survived such an exodus as a child. The memories of loved ones starving, of the harsh insensitive treatment of his people, still haunted him. It was his desire for retribution for the atrocities against his people that kindled the fire that drove him to believe in the cause of the SLP.

He picked up his tickets and made his way toward the gate. As he passed through security he thought of how easy it had proven to foil these "rent-a-cops." Security in U.S. airports was famous throughout the terrorists networks for its weakness. The terrorist organizations had unanimously agreed not to provoke a tightening of this security by initiating attacks against them. The American airports were far too vital to the underground networks that trafficked in a variety of goods required to support the cause. Better that the Americans remain asleep, so that the cause could be furthered elsewhere.

Farouk had no fear as he moved through the metal detector. The high temperature plastic weapon which was concealed in his jacket had less metal in it than a twenty-five cent piece. Even the cartridges were made of plastic, with special ceramic slugs. It would take years for the security industry to come up with a means of detecting this kind of weapon.

Once again, a consensus among the terrorist organizations, not to use such weapons in the commission of acts of air piracy, was designed to keep the sleeping security infrastructure unaware that they were being violated at will.

Farouk boarded the aircraft and looked out at the reddish sunset. He was on the prowl now. He was seeking an animal that was not used to being hunted. He was sure that the chase would be easy, and that the kill would be swift. He closed the shade on his window and closed his eyes. He had learned two very important laws of survival in this game, eat whenever you can because you don't know when you will eat again, and rest for the same reason. Farouk had learned these and other, more deadly lessons, as well.

May 23, 19:00 EDT

As Farouk's plane ascended into the darkening evening sky, Special Agent Eugene Randall was putting the finishing touches on the plan to raid the known SLP member locations. Dressed in a Kevlar vest and the renowned blue FBI caps and jackets, Randall's team was interspersed with the few local law enforcement agents that the FBI could muster. Randall had also received permission to use a U.S. Army "Delta" team. Even more elite than the famous "Special Forces," the Delta teams primary *raison de etre* was counter terrorism activities.

Because the identities of Delta team members was a well-guarded secret, the team had been briefed separately and was now in position around the SLP headquarters. Each member wore a dark face mask very similar to those worn by members of their British counterparts in the Special Air Services. While Randall appreciated all the help he could get, the Delta team made him extremely nervous.

"Alright, I want everyone in positions within 5 minutes. Mike I want you to signal the perimeter teams that the area is hot and that anyone trying to enter or exit the areas are to be detained," Randall said, as he turned from the tactical maps that covered the wall of the makeshift operations center.

"Okay, G," Mike replied. "I also have the prints from the surveillance film we shot this morning. Here's the guy I was telling you about."

Mike handed the picture of Farouk to Randall. Randall scrutinized it and then handed it back. "Make sure that a copy of this photo gets faxed to all of the team leaders. Make sure that the Port Authority and airport security get the picture as well, with orders to detain, and a warning that he should be considered extremely dangerous. Also make sure that we get a copy back to the safe house to see if our friend can give us a line on this guy. There's something familiar about him but I can't quite place it."

Mike nodded acknowledgment and headed to the communications center. He wanted to make sure that he had completed the task assigned to him before the raid commenced. "This is one show I don't want to miss," he thought to himself as he hurried off.

Randall excused the rest of the members and left the operations center which was located across from the SLP headquarters. All access to the headquarters had been from the far side of the building and could not be detected by the unwitting occupants of the SLP headquarters. Randall moved toward a plain dark blue van and entered the back. As he entered two individuals dressed in FBI garb emerged out of the shadows.

"Listen guys, this thing is going down in about a half hour. About five minutes after the bust goes down and the area is declared safe, I want you to move this van up to the door on the East side. You've got your plan in place, right?"

One of the men in FBI garb nodded acknowledgment. Agent Randall didn't know it, but this was the same man who had been placed on guard outside of the NYSE the night that Evan and Dave had been working on the computer virus there. Had Randall known what this man and his associate were capable of he would have another set of individuals that made him "extremely" uncomfortable.

Randall turned and left the van. Even though he didn't know anything about the two individuals appointed to oversee the planting of the computer equipment in the SLP headquarters, they gave him an uneasy feeling. Randall had learned long ago not to ask too many questions of the individuals he met during "inter-agency" actions. But he had met similar characters, on more than one occasion.

Suddenly Randall's ear piece crackled. "This is post two. We've apprehended two male suspects attempting to exit the area."

Randall spoke into his headset, "This is team leader. Restrain them and evacuate them from the area. Twenty minutes until H hour. Good job, position two."

Randall headed to the communications center to check on Mike. He had a deep affection for Zvaboda and knew that Mike wanted to be in on the bust. As he approached another, larger, van, the door at the back opened and Mike stepped out. Randall grinned a bright white grin that made him look like the Cheshire cat in the half light of the few sodium street lamps.

"Damn G, you look like the cat that ate the canary," Mike said, smiling at his partners mischievous smile.

"Just checkin' on you. Thought we might have to start without you."

Mike produced an exaggerated frown. "Now you wouldn't let me miss out on the fun, would you?"

Randall smiled even wider, "Nah, you spent too much time on this one. Wouldn't want you to miss the payoff."

"Good," Mike answered, "I got those pictures off and also sent it to the Identification Center so we might be able to get a handle on this guy."

"Great, let's get over into position. You heard about the two guys they brought down over on the east side, right?"

"Yeah, I thought I could hear the Delta team interrogator salivating. The Delta leader already dispatched him on their TAC channel. I don't know if I can get used to those guys G."

"I know what you mean. There's not a hell of a lot we can do though. Orders came down from 'very' high up on this one."

Randall and Zvaboda headed into the building that housed the operations center. They passed through the building's first floor by following a trail of luminescent markers that eliminated the need to navigate the treacherous passage with flashlights. This was just another technique in the Delta team's bag of tricks. It was meant to keep the bad guys unaware of their impending fate. Randall made a note to himself that perhaps the FBI should adopt a similar method for this kind of operation.

As Randall and Zvaboda neared the side of the building facing the SLP headquarters, they used available cover to avoid detection in the dim light that seeped through the broken windows of the building. They took up their positions with some fellow FBI agents near the doorway which was directly across from the SLP headquarters.

The plan that Randall had devised was for the quicker, quieter Delta team to enter the abandoned areas of the building using their night vision devices. They would then coordinate their movement toward the populated areas of the building with the law enforcement personnel on the outside. This coordination would culminate in the storming of the front of the building as the Delta teams covered the actions of the terrorists from key vantage points.

May 23, 20:00 EDT

Eric Hawkins, enjoyed being a Delta team leader. He had had a long and distinguished career in the Army as a member of the elite Ranger Battalion in Ft. Lewis Washington. His love for adventure and skydiving, combined with his exemplary performance with the Rangers had led to his recruitment as a member of the Delta forces. Through hard work and diligence he had finally received leadership over a team of his own. He had taken this team and honed it into a finely tuned fighting machine that worked as a single entity. Each member was sensitized to the situation of each other member. Creating an unexplainable link that had served to help them survive more than one close encounter.

This mission seemed straight forward to the Delta team, and yet their collective psyche had a bad feeling about it. The fear was unspoken, yet each team member knew that the others felt the impending danger. Obviously none could tell what dread result would come of the mission. The not knowing, combined with the certainty that "something" was going to happen made everybody tense.

Hawkins moved the members of the team into position. He looked at his black-faced, luminescent watch. Its design was simple and practical. He watched the sweep second hand traverse the face once, then twice. As the second hand reached the top of the face the second time, Hawkins gave the whisper like hand signals that moved his team into the building.

The team entered the building like a silent, unseen shadow. Their night vision devices were far more sophisticated than those used by normal combat troops, like those in operation Desert Storm. They were low profile, and presented a much more detailed picture for the viewer. This detail was vital in terrorist operations, where booby traps needed to be detected, and hostages needed to be distinguished from threats.

The team members marked their approach on the target by keying their microphones. The radios they used sent a digital signal that identified the sender. This digital signal appeared as a station number on a computer display for daytime operations, and onto the corner of the night viewing devices for night time operations.

Eric watched the progress of his team and when everyone had signaled arrival at their next checkpoint he would key his mike signaling them to continue.

The team's approach on the terrorists went flawlessly. The design of the building was such that there was a series of catwalks which encircled and crossed the open first floor area. This area had been identified as the area used by the SLP. The Delta team was to secure this upper level of catwalks and then make sure that the first floor entry teams were not threatened as they entered the building.

The team members moved into final position. They had explicit orders not to shoot unless a hostile action was detected. The way they were feeling, Hawkins wondered what could be considered a hostile action. He hoped he wouldn't have to go through mounds of paperwork because some damned terrorist went for a cigarette lighter. With this unsettling thought, Erik made himself comfortable and waited for the fireworks to begin.

A Delta team liaison officer had been watching the progress of the team in a special operations van. From this van the officer could not only monitor the communications of the team to watch their progress, he could also watch the actual positions of the team members because of special locator devices which were a part of each team members communications system. The liaison officer noted that all the members had reached their assigned locations, he relayed this information to Randall via the joint operations frequency.

Randall looked at his watch. Twenty minutes had transpired since he had briefed and released the team members. The Delta team had started its operation five minutes after that time, Randall checked with the communications center to make sure that the other locations around the city were ready. This sweep was designed to capture all known SLP members with one fell swoop.

So far, reports indicated that there was only one man unaccounted for, the mysterious man that Mike had photographed leaving the headquarters that morning. Randall had a bad feeling about that guy, but one person out of 150 could not cause the operation to stall.

Randall gave the "PROCEED ACCORDING TO PLAN" message when there were five minutes remaining until H hour. This message was the mark for the five minute countdown, and except for urgent communications, radio silence was instituted.

Hawkins heard Randall's message. He readied himself and peered through the sights of his scope. He and one other team member were the designated shooters. They each had an area of responsibility. Their mission was to insure that the other team members were free to secure their designated sections without fear of other threats. The shooters were the "Big Picture" guys, responsible for controlling the whole situation.

As H hour neared, Hawkins readied his weapon and watched the second hand of his watch drag across the face. Time seemed to slow down as H hour approached. Hawkins was thankful for this. He and his team members had an ability to turn their world into a slow motion event, similar to a Sam Peckinpaw movie. This was a result of the accelerated thought processes required for survival in life and death situations. Hawkins and his team waited in a time warp that was no less real than those theorized by Einstein.

As the second hand made its slow sojourn from the last tick to the top of the face. Hawkins took careful account of the environment. At the same moment Randall's teams began their rapid approach on the building. H hour came and several flash grenades were released by Delta team members. The SLP members were stunned by the bright lights and noise that these grenades produced. As the terrorists tried to ascertain the nature of the explosions, and recover their faculties, the Delta team members moved over the rails of the catwalks and slid down to the first floor. They quickly forced each SLP member in their respective areas to the ground. The FBI members broke down the front door and started to sweep toward the Delta team members. There was no resistance on the part of the SLP members, so quick and undetected had been the attack.

Unbeknownst to any of the members of the arrest team, Ibrahim had quickly ascertained the situation and had discreetly pressed an unseen button under his desk. As the members of the Delta team moved toward him, he quickly moved to the door, confident that the will of Allah would be done, through the small act of pressing that small button.

The SLP members were quickly rounded up.

While the speed and success of the roundup was unquestioned. The speed with which the electrical impulse that Ibrahim had triggered traveled much faster. The impulse was a quick burst of a computer message that went through a shielded, undocumented telephone line, that the law enforcement officials had no idea existed. The electrical burst was recognized immediately by ENCHANTRESS which had infected the New York City telephone switching center. The ENCHANTRESS relayed the bursts to the operations center in New Mexico which caused Jasmina's displays to light up.

Jasmina quickly determined the reason for the urgent electronic appeal for help. The computer system suggested a retaliatory response in kind, and Jasmina quickly authorized the execution of the plan. Within minutes of the arrest of the SLP members in New York, retribution had be meted out.

May 23, 17:00 PDT

Steve Anders had been a process control engineer responsible for the manufacture of chlorine for swimming pools in a suburban Los Angles plant for several years. He loved process control and computers. His pastimes included running a bulletin board system in his spare time. Many times Steve would take work home, transferring the data onto floppy disks between his home computer and the one at work. It was this mechanism that caused the computer system that was used to control the manufacture and storage of more than 50 tons of chlorine to become infected.

ENCHANTRESS had quickly ascertained that the infected PDP-11/73 process control computer had a communications port to allow remote support of the system. The program gathered what information it could about the system and then called NECROMANCER to apprise her of the situation.

Jasmina had quickly realized the value of the enchantment of the process control computer and had put it upon her list of targets of opportunity, At 5 pm Pacific Daylight Time the PDP-11/73 received a very brief telephone call that would severely impact the Southern LA area. The call had been instigated as a result of the arrests of the New York SLP members.

Within a matter of 60 seconds after the telephone call, the entire 50 tons of compressed, gaseous chlorine stored at the facility was released into the atmosphere. The storage tanks of hydrochloric acid on the site were also spilled. The spill of this acid served to further damage the plant and to hinder the efforts of anyone who might survive the sudden release of chlorine in their attempt to try and stop the flow manually.

Unfortunately, the release of the hydrochloric acid had not been needed. All twelve of the personnel in the control room for the chlorine storage facility were completely overcome before they could get into their emergency response gear, Because the night shift had just come on, there had been few other personnel on plant site, except for janitorial personnel who were moving through the administration buildings doing their nightly chores. They never knew what hit them. The stinging and choking sensation felt 100,000 times more powerful than that caused from swimming in a heavily chlorinated pool.

Overcome immediately, no survivors were found.

The huge greenish cloud drifted in a easterly direction. Damage to personnel and property diminished as the chlorine concentration dissipated. Unfortunately, the concentration had not reduced significantly before it crossed the Santa Ana freeway. The total casualties from the ensuing wrecks, and respiratory failures climbed over 100 by the time the local emergency response team could evacuate the affected areas and cordon off access to them.

The final death toll from the Chlorine Catastrophe would finally climb to 263 deaths, and another 500 people with irreparable respiratory damage. Minutes after the chlorine release a call was received from a national voice mail system in Omaha, Nebraska to the CNN newsroom in Atlanta. The message was short and ominous- "The members arrested in New York City were innocent in the Times Square Tragedy. The longer they stay in jail the more people who would suffer like those in Los Angeles."

May 24, 05:00 EDT

Farouk awoke early. He quickly washed and readied himself for morning prayers. Farouk's religion had been a constant support to him. His avid love of Allah and belief in the ways of Islam gave him an inner peace that sustained him through all the adversities that he had known in his life. He felt exhilarated after prayers, knowing that the God that had conquered most of Europe once, and who promised a place in heaven for those that died for the cause, had heard his prayers and was watching over him.

Farouk turned on Headline News to see what was happening in the world. He turned up the volume so that he could hear the broadcast as he shaved and readied himself in his quest for Evan Smith, the accursed infidel who had stopped the SLP's attack on the New York Stock Exchange.

Farouk turned on the hot water and filled the basin. Using a shaving brush he worked a thick lather onto his face, letting the lather soften his bristles. He then withdrew an ominous straight razor and ran it across a strop several times to hone the edge. He pulled the razor across his face with the precision of a surgeon, listening to the latest news of world events.

Suddenly, news of the SLP arrests in New York came on.

Farouk paused and moved to the television to see what he could ascertain from the video tape coverage. He saw his brothers in the cause being paraded into large police vans. The film crew showed a van full of computer equipment which had supposedly been seized during the raid. This lie infuriated Farouk. He understood the attempt to convince the public that the perpetrators of the Times Square Tragedy had been apprehended. Immediately afterward came an in-depth report of the Chlorine Catastrophe which had occurred last evening.

He thanked Allah that someone in the raid had been able to get off a distress signal. He also thanked Allah that he had been able to get free to pursue this Evan Smith. Allah was truly wise. No infidels would be able to circumvent his will.

Farouk moved back to the bathroom and finished shaving. Thinking of the blows he would strike in retaliation for this interference with the SLP plans. Americans would soon know suffering like they had never known it before.

Boston's rich heritage and historic importance did not interest him. This city was a mere infant compared to the cities of the Middle East. The whole country and its occupants were nothing more than lucky young dolts. He despised America and its support of the filthy Jews who hid here, supporting the bastard nation of Israel.

Were it not for American and British meddling Israel and every Jew in it would have been destroyed long ago. It was time to teach these wet behind the ears Americans the cost of backing the Jews. Farouk contemplated the elimination of Evan Smith and anyone else that might stop the retribution that had been planned. He relished the thought of removing these stumbling blocks from Allah's path.

Farouk went downstairs and ate a hearty breakfast. He read the newspaper and drank a second cup of coffee while he waited for time to pass. The Alumni offices did not open until 9:00 and he did not want to show up too early. Patience was another skill that he had learned in his years as a hunter of men. It had served him well on many occasions.

After enough time had passed, Farouk left the restaurant and retrieved his rental car. He made the drive to Cambridge and found the MIT Alumni Association offices easily.

He parked the car and got out.

He was dressed in an expensive Italian suit and black Italian shoes. He carried credentials identifying him as a freelance writer of Ziff-Davis. Ziff-Davis was well known in computer circles for their series of publications covering virtually every aspect of the computer world. As he entered the offices he was greeted by a young receptionist.

"May I help you?"

"Yes," Farouk answered, smiling a disarming smile. "My name is Michael Ferris, I freelance for Ziff-Davis publications. I'm doing a story on artificial computer intelligence and came across a doctoral thesis by an alumni named Evan Smith. I was wondering if I might find Dr. Smith to see what has become of him and his theories."

The young lady beamed, happy that this was a simple request that she could easily fulfill for the handsome gentleman. "We have a directory of all alumni, if you'll take a seat over there, I'll get it for you," she said pointing to a study table in a reading area to one side.

Farouk smiled and thanked her. His demeanor did not betray the fact that he was on a mission to drain the life of another man. Nor did it show the wear of the hundreds of men that he had killed before.

He sat down at the dark mahogany table and turned on the brass study lamp. The young receptionist quickly returned with an alumni directory.

"This is the locator directory. If you are interested in biographical data or other accomplishments I'd be happy to retrieve Dr. Smith's data," she said as she placed the directory next to Farouk.

"Thank you," Farouk replied, "but I've some very special questions to ask Mr. Smith and talking to him will be better than trying to delve through all the biographical data. I'm behind deadline on this and I need to interview him as soon as possible."

The receptionist smiled and left Farouk with the directory, He quickly copied down the required information and returned the directory to the receptionist at her desk.

"Thank you, you were most helpful."

"My pleasure Mr. Ferris. Actually it can get pretty boring around here."

Farouk frowned. "Well, it's a shame that I've got this story to do or I would suggest that we go out and you could show me the town."

The receptionist smiled, flattered that such an attractive man would be so straight forward with her. "Well maybe next time you're in town?"

"I certainly hope so. Thanks again for the help. I'll look you up next time I'm in town."

With that, Farouk exit the offices and headed to a pay phone. He dialed an access code that the ENCHANTRESS of the Cambridge phone system recognized as a request for voice communications with the operations center in New Mexico.

Jasmina and her staff of programmers had been hard at work adapting ENCHANTRESS for each system that it had found. Part of the process of the full-fledged ENCHANTRESS infection was adaptation to exploit the computer system that had been infected. Thus, the telephone company ENCHANTRESS infections watched for certain codes and then acted upon those codes before the telephone switching system ever got into the game. This was the same means which had been employed in the transmittal of the distress signal from the New York cell.

Within seconds Farouk was in touch with the command center in New Mexico. "This is Farouk, I must speak to Ibn"

Ibn quickly came to the phone. They had been uncertain of Farouk's whereabouts and were glad to have contact with him.

"Farouk, where are you, did you get out of New York safely?"

"I'm in Cambridge, getting ready to leave for Baltimore. I need arrangements made. I also need to know if it is safe for me to fly or if I will have to drive."

"Jasmina has been scanning the computer traffic for any sign of activity concerning you. She has not seen anything that indicates that they know who you are or where you are. The last indication we have of you is in a security alert for the New York City area. As long as you don't fly through there you should be safe."

"I will make arrangements for you to fly into Baltimore Washington International. What name are you traveling under?"

"I'm traveling under my Michael Ferris id. I flew Delta up here so that's probably the most logical choice for flying out."

"Okay, I'll have the tickets waiting for you at the counter."

Farouk hung up the phone and went to the car. He could taste the kill. Nothing would assuage his appetite for revenge on this Evan Smith for his meddling. His hatred was pure. It had been refined and distilled in his youth. He had learned to use his hate as his most valuable weapon. A weapon that caused any compassion to be squelched, any concern for his safety to be hidden in the dark blackness of this pure emotion.

May 24, 15:00 EDT

Hawkins and his team could not have known that the slight motion made by the terrorist named Ibrahim would have such a catastrophic effect. They all realized that somehow a distress signal had be sent through the seemingly impenetrable gauntlet that had been thrown up around the terrorists. But the method of alarm had not been readily apparent.

The telephone lines that had been identified had been cut seconds before the raid began. It had taken more than two hours to identify the mechanism that had allowed the terrorists to make their distress call.

The team had had a bad feeling about this one. But the damage afflicted upon civilians as a result of the raid had been so quick and dramatic that it had shocked everyone.

Hawkins and his team were sitting in their quarters waiting for some tangible intelligence to come out of the interrogation and intelligence analysis so that they could react immediately. The Chlorine Catastrophe was taken as a personal insult to the professionalism of Hawkins' team. They all wanted to catch the terrorists who had committed this heinous act.

Until the culprits were captured Hawkins' team was on "lock-in" a military euphemism for forced confinement. All the Delta team could do was sit and wait for the terrorists to be located so that they could rectify the situation.

A few miles away, Eugene Randall and Mike Zvaboda were sitting in Eugene's room in the Bachelor's Officers

Quarters (BOQ). Randall could not stop to appreciate the heavily wooded scenery that made up Fort Bragg. His impatience with this waiting game, and his extreme irritation with the Chlorine Catastrophe made futile any attempt to relax.

Randall was standing at the window with his second highball looking in the general direction of the interrogation facility. Deep frustration filled his soul. "Damn I hate this waiting."

Mike was drinking a Corona. A beer he had learned to enjoy during his assignment in Houston. He too had been disappointed by the fact that the terrorists had been able to get their deadly distress signal through the net that had been thrown down around the terrorists. They had been able to track down the contact in the telephone company who had accommodated the fatal telephone link that had circumvented all the precautions that the team had taken but only after the illicit line had been used to kill and maim hundreds.

"G, we did everything we could. At least we got the SOB at the telephone company."

"I know, but we've got to take these guys out. They're creating panic, havoc, and committing crimes at will. These sons of bitches have got to be caught. It's like the 20's all over again."

Suddenly the phone rang, Mike reached over and answered it.

"Hello. Yeah he's here. Just a second."

Mike looked up at Randall. "It's the Joint Intelligence Center."

Randall perked up, anxious to have a breakthrough. He took the phone from Mike.

"Randall here."

He listened for a few seconds. "I understand. Great, we'll be right over."

Randall hung up the phone. He smiled at Mike. Mike had forgotten how long it had been since he had seen that smile, It seemed like forever but he knew that it had only been a matter of probably 24 hours.

The whole sequence of events that had taken place after the raids had seemed like a blurred dream. They had spent nearly two hours gathering every piece of physical evidence that was readily available at the headquarters and had moved that evidence along with all of the prisoners onto Military C5A Starlifter aircraft.

They had landed at Ft. Bragg and quickly allocated quarters and implemented the interrogation/ intelligence analysis plan that had been devised. It had been only 20 hours since the raid. Yet, it seemed like it had been much longer.

Randall looked at Mike. "Get your jacket, they've come up with something at the JIC."

Mike rose and grabbed his jacket and sunglasses. They headed out the door got in the car and headed for the JIC.

May 24, 15:00 EDT

Farouk had picked up his tickets at the Delta counter and had made the flight to Baltimore without a hitch. When he landed at BWI he picked up an envelope at the reservations counter. In the envelope was a key to a late model Ford Mustang, and directions to the car. The Baltimore cell of the SLP had not been infiltrated and it had been agreed that they would minimize their participation with Farouk's operations to avoid detection.

Farouk crossed the parking lot and found the Mustang easily. He opened the trunk and saw the materials that he had requested Ibn acquire for him. He put his flight bag in the trunk and then got into the car. He opened the map of Baltimore that he had purchased in the airport and found the area he was looking for. He smiled to himself as he adjusted his mirrors and started the car.

He knew that he was close now. Nothing would stop him from accomplishing his mission.

May 24, 18:00 EDT

Randall and Zvaboda arrived in at the JIC and cleared security. They immediately went to the conference room that served as the operations center. They were greeted by several intelligence analysts and Jim Carter the JIC leader. Carter knew Randall from their days together in the FBI and smiled when he saw Randall walk in.

"G, it's been a long time," Carter said as he moved toward Randall with his hand extended.

"Jim you haven't aged a day. I hear you guys have got a break."

"Yeah, I guess we'll have to catch up on lost time some other time. We've been interrogating the principle people and have come up with a disturbing development."

"You remember this guy?," Carter asked, showing Randall and Zvaboda a picture of Farouk.

Mike spoke up. "Yeah that's the guy we made leaving the SLP headquarters."

"That's right," Carter continued. "His name is Farouk. We were able to get that much from your informant, although he had no idea what this guy did."

"We've been using a variety of chemical interrogation techniques because of the limited amount of time that we have. The cell leader, Ibrahim, was able to give us a very complete biography on this guy. Although I don't think he'll ever remember telling us a thing when we bring him out. Seems this guy is heavy muscle for the SLP. He specializes in 'wet' operations."

"I didn't think these guys were into that kind of thing," Randall interjected. "Our informant said they were more technically oriented."

"That's true," Carter answered. "However, it seems that Farouk was sent as a backup by the PLO in case these guys needed it. Well it seems that since you guys stopped the NYSE incident from happening this guy has got his marching orders."

"Who's his target?," Mike asked.

"Before I tell you that, I want you to know that this situation is being taken care of as we speak. Our friends from the raid are heading down to provide protection now. They were deemed the most capable of handling this situation without spooking the target."

"Well?," Randall replied, anxious to know what was going on.

"It seems that they made a guy named Evan Smith as being one of the guys at the NYSE. They got orders from very high up to eliminate him."

"Smith," Randall said. "Yeah, I remember him. Seemed to be pretty squared away."

"He's gotta be more than squared away," Jim continued. "As soon as the big guys got this information they went fitty. I don't know who this guy is but he must be real important."

"So we know where one bad guy is," Mike broke in. "What have your wonder drugs brought up about the real nerve center these guys have set up?"

"That's why I really called you guys down here. Seems that none of our prisoners knew anything about the main cell except that they were somewhere in New

Mexico. However, we do have some joint information that made the ballpark much smaller to play in. I can't tell you what intelligence was involved. But I can tell you where the ballpark is. It was a result of your tip a few days ago, as a matter of fact G."

"So where is it Jim?," Randall asked his excitement becoming uncontrollable.

Jim smiled. "Still the same old go get 'em G, aren't you?"

Carter motioned to a topographical map laying on the desk in front of them. "It's in the area of Escondido mountain," he continued, pointing to an elevation of 9,869 feet in the western most part of the state. "We've got everyone headed here so that they can come up with an attack plan."

Randall looked at Mike. "Why don't you see if you can get a number for Dominoes? I think it's gonna be a long night and thinkin' always makes me hungry."

Mike smiled. "You got it boss."

Evan was rudely awakened by a knocking on his townhouse door. When he looked at his alarm clock he saw that it was 2:30 in the morning. He stumbled across the bedroom looking for his robe. He found it and tied it as he moved downstairs to the front door.

He turned on the front porch light and peered through the peephole. He immediately recognized one of the men who had been standing guard at the NYSE. One of the same men who had been in the FBI garb that had helped plant the computer equipment at the FBI raid in New York (although Smith was not aware of the man's involvement in that operation).

Evan cracked the door, leaving the security chain on. "Do you know what time it is?"

"Dr. Smith, we need to come in before anyone notices us. We'll explain when we get out of the street."

For the first time in his long intelligence career, Evan felt physically in danger. He immediately opened the door and two agents entered. He quickly secured the door when they were inside.

The first agent moved Evan toward the center of the building, using his own body as a shield to the exterior walls.

The second agent withdrew an Ingram MAC-10 from a shoulder holster and turned off the living room lights. He made himself comfortable in a position where he could watch the exterior of the building.

"What the hell is going on?" Evan asked, his voiced wavering with a subtle hint of fear.

"Dr. Smith," the first agent answered. "You need to call Dr. Sanders. I have a secure phone and it will take a few minutes to set it up. I know that you trust him and it's probably better that you talk to him instead of me about this."

Evan was somewhat calmed by the agent's calm and professional manner. He had never had much opportunity to talk to these guys and always thought they probably had difficulty pronouncing words with more than two syllables in them. It now occurred to him how stupid it had been for him to prejudge anyone.

Within a few minutes the secure phone was connected and Evan was talking to Paul. "Paul, what the hell is going on? Where are you?"

"Evan I'm at home same as you. They found out that there is a very real threat to your life and possibly mine and Dave's as well. All I can tell you is that you need to listen to your security team and try not to let this thing shake you too much."

"Jeez Paul, what did we get ourselves into? Death threats, people dying left and right, this isn't the job I signed up for."

"I know Evan. The good news is that this thing should be over soon. They've just about nailed these guys."

"Okay, Paul, gonna try and get some shuteye. How do I handle getting to work?"

"Your security team will take care of it. Don't worry Evan these guys really are the best."

Evan hung up the phone and addressed the agents. "Sorry I was so sharp with you guys. I'm always a little cranky when I wake up. Make yourselves at home and I want you to know I appreciate you guys being here."

The agents gave Evan a reassuring look that had a hint of thanks in it. They were not used to thanks from the people they protected. They were ostracized even more than the people in COMPOPS.

Thanks was a nice thing to hear.

Evan moved up to bed and finished sleeping. He did not sleep extremely well.

May 25, 05:30 EDT

Farouk had slept until about four in the morning and then had readied himself for the kill. The previous day he had determined the make, model and license number of Evan Smith's car from the Bureau of Motor Vehicles. He made his way to the area of Evan Smith's home. He parked the car so that he was not observable from the townhouse, but so that he could plainly see Evan Smith's car. He waited patiently for his prey, the tinted windows of the Mustang concealing his presence.

At 5:30 a tall sandy-haired man came out of the door of Smith's townhouse. Farouk readied the RPG-7 that was sitting beside him in the passenger seat. As the man disabled the car alarm and started to unlock his car, Farouk stepped quickly out of the car, aimed, and fired the RPG at the gas tank, The ensuing explosion lifted the man off of the ground and threw him several feet into the air. Farouk discarded the RPG and released the Uzi from its shoulder holster. He moved quickly toward his prey to make sure of the kill.

Farouk was surprised by a sudden explosion from the townhouse door. Before he could react one of the agents that had appeared at Evan Smith's door the night before unloaded a full magazine into the trained killer. It was an exceedingly tight shot group. One that was designed to overwhelm typical body armor.

Of the thirty Teflon coated shells that pierced Farouk's body, twenty-seven had been in a three inch circle around the heart. The other three had been placed cleanly in the head.

The agent dashed madly for the body near the flaming car. He lifted the body in a fireman's carry and moved the body quickly back into the townhouse. The agent got on the secure line and made a quick phone call. "This is JAGUAR we have an ALPHA emergency, I need assistance NOW!"

May 25, 15:00 EDT

Paul Sanders walked into the clean room as Dave turned around to see who was coming in. He knew that he was safe his two "Goons" were firmly implanted in front of the clean room door. They scared the bejesus out of him but he felt safe.

Dave knew that something was wrong when he saw the expression on Paul's face. They had all been through a lot in the last few weeks, but the look was even more haggard than usual.

"What's wrong Paul?"

"Dave, it's Evan. The nut they sent after him got to him early this morning. Evan's security team got the guy, but not until after he blew Evan's car to pieces."

"Is he..."

Paul looked down to the floor. The loss of a dear friend was obvious. "Yes, he's dead. They thought that he might make it. The son of a bitch blew up Evan's car and was going to make sure that he'd killed Evan when the security team got him. They sent Evan to Johns Hopkins trauma via life flight, but he was dead before they landed."

Dave was speechless. It had been Evan as much as Paul who had helped to get Dave off of the third floor. He had valued Evan's help and support. Evan's loss hit Dave hard.

"The funeral is going to be tomorrow. It'll be closed casket because of the damage done by the explosion. I know that Evan would have wanted you to be there."

Dave looked tearfully at Paul. "Thanks Paul, I'll be there. Listen I know how close you and Evan were. I just want you to know that I'm terribly sorry."

Paul looked at Dave thankfully and exited. He went upstairs followed by his security team and boarded a helicopter for the White House, he and the President had some very important things to discuss.

May 27, 14:00 EDT

Paul and the President had just finished discussing the implementation of the JAGERMIESTER project. As Paul was getting ready to leave a senior member of the National Security Council barged in. "Mr. President, I'm sorry to intrude but we have another emergency and Mr. Sander's presence is most fortuitous."

The President grimaced. The current situation had taken its toll upon him as well. He prayed that JAGERMIESTER combined with the FBI Joint Task force would finally end this nightmare before his constitution was completely drained.

"What is it Jean?"

The NSC member described the situation. "It seems that at 1:30 PM the Federal Reserve system computers started to be inundated with bogus messages. These messages have bogged down the whole system to the point that money has literally stopped flowing."

Paul gasped a deep gasp. The impact of this latest attack shook Paul to the bone. Unless the valid message traffic could be separated from the bogus messages, transactions couldn't be processed.

Furthermore, infection of systems that had access to the Federal Reserve system, meant that seemingly valid messages could also be created that could move millions of dollars through the system without authorization.

The President looked at Paul. He did not know the technical implications. He did know the financial implications. The Federal Reserve system is the means of verifying and accomplishing transactions between banks around the country. Without the computer system the entire monetary system would slow to a trickle. "Paul get your people on this NOW! I want to know how long it's going to take to clean up this mess. Report back to me by 5:00."

"I'll do my best Mr. President. This is sort of a twist, as the Federal Reserve system computers aren't the problem. It's all the computers that are talking to it."

"I don't care what it takes Paul. You get your people on this and let me know what you need. Jean you go with Paul and bring him up to date with what's going on."

The NSC member and Paul headed out the door to combat the newest terrorist attack. The President leaned back in his chair and rubbed his temples. This crisis was taking its toll on everyone involved.

May 27, 19:00 CDT

Agent Randall had received a coded dispatch while the two C5A Starlifters were in the air headed toward Kirtland Air Force Base in New Mexico. It described in detail the newest crisis. It also cautioned him to recover as much information as possible intact to aid in undoing the damage that had been sown by the ENCHANTRESS. Dave Anderson would take a military flight from Andrews Air Force Base to Kirtland and meet them when things were under control.

Because of the sensitivity of the operation, and because of the previous compromise of COMPOPS personnel, it was decided that COMPOPS personnel should not be on the scene until the area was completely secured. Randall had heard the reports of the unfortunate incident with Smith. While he did not know the man, he did appreciate the loss of a person that seemed to be a key to defeating this menace.

Evan would have been going to New Mexico instead of Dave, but that was no longer possible. The rest of Dave's team was being hurriedly packed up and shipped off to the Federal Reserve System Computer Center where they would hopefully stop the attacks on the nation's money supply.

The flight to Kirtland was somber. The members of the task force were mainly those people who had been in on the New York raid. The contingent had been bolstered by more Delta team members and FBI personnel to make up for the loss of local law enforcement personnel who had been available in New York.

Randall was the titular head of the operation. He was bolstered in this capacity by Hawkins, who helped to make the tactical combat strategy. The combination of talents helped to make a strong team that had been extremely effective in the operation in New York. Hawkins and his team were on the same plane as Randall and Zvaboda.

Tied to the main floor of the huge aircraft were Army HMMWV vehicles. The successor to the standard Jeep. These wide flat four wheel drive vehicles were all rigged with advanced radio communications gear and would provide the means for maneuvering on the ground once they arrived at the operational area.

They would land at Kirtland and the Delta team members would then transfer to smaller C130's that would paradrop the teams over the area. Local law enforcement had already been contacted and asked to cordon off the area. However, the road blocks were put up with the cover of searching for escaped convicts. The local law enforcement agents were given explicit orders not to try to apprehend any of the Palestinian suspects.

The Delta teams were to search for the hideout and tighten the noose on the suspects, while the rest of the task force motored in with the HMMWV's and support vehicles. They were to reconnoiter the area and prepare a strategy for seizing the site with minimal damage to the suspects and more importantly to their facility and equipment.

It was 8:00 in the evening when the Task Force landed at Kirtland. Randall went over last minute notes with Hawkins and representatives of the other agencies involved. The Delta team members grabbed their parachutes and headed toward the C130 turboprop aircraft. They were dressed in black jumpsuits and had pulled black masks over their faces to disguise themselves from unindoctrinated personnel. On their hands they wore black tight fitting gloves that helped to camouflage their skin color. To Randall it looked like a line of solid black automatons.

In the reddening sky of the New Mexico dusk the sight of the task force assembling on the tarmac was haunting. It gave Randall a chill when he thought of the weaponry and personnel required to thwart a bunch of "computer nerds." These terrorists had hit the jugular vein of the information society and with deadly results.

May 28, 10:00 EDT

The turnout for Evan Smith's funeral was very small. Less than a dozen people stood around the casket. Paul and Dave stood solemnly staring at the casket in the light drizzle. Evan's mother and father stood at the graveside. Mary, Evan's sometime secretary, was there as well. It wasn't that more people didn't want to attend. Rather, Evan's funeral had been made an extremely closed affair. The turnout was further diminished by the fact that there was a frenzy of activity at COMPOPS, between trying to thwart the newest terrorist attack, and the preparation of the JAGERMIESTER release tapes. Because of the diminished turnout, and the extreme concern for security, the security team, covering the perimeter from a discrete distance, outnumbered the funeral party by five.

Paul stared at the casket as the minister delivered the eulogy. The overcast sky, and light drizzle seemed to emphasize the somber tone of the occasion.

This was the first casualty that COMPOPS had incurred in its history.

No one could have foreseen this tragedy.

COMPOPS was a new generation of intelligence collection, far removed from the cloak and dagger activities of its sister agencies.

The whole concept of COMPOPS was to acquire high quality data with no risk to human agents. Paul knew that he should have anticipated some loss of life. COMPOPS' closest counterpart, the National Security Agency, had suffered casualties, despite the fact that they were tasked with pulling intelligence from the ether in the form of radio transmissions.

Still, COMPOPS did not require that its operators be in close proximity to its targets, as was required in some radio intelligence operations. While Evan's demise had not been the direct result of his intelligence collecting activities, it was a direct result of the enemies identification of Evan and his abilities as a direct threat to their terrorist activities.

Paul regretted the fact that Evan's death had occurred from his identification as a member of the group responsible for thwarting the terrorists' attempts. At the same time he felt confident that the COMPOPS agency itself remained undiscovered. It was one thing to identify an individual, quite another to identify an entire organization and its mission.

As the funeral came to a close, Paul stopped his inner reflection. There was no time to dwell upon what might have been. If Evan's death were to count for anything, Paul knew that the JAGERMIESTER project must be completed without delay. He entered his government limousine and immediately made a phone call to his secretary. She assured him that all the individuals whose presence had been requested had been contacted and that they all had confirmed that they would attend. With that, Paul directed his driver to make a quick detour before heading for the conference site.

May 28, 13:30 EDT

Paul Sanders looked at the gentlemen seated around the conference table. These were the same gentlemen who had been forewarned about the upcoming software changes that were to be issued. Each person had a large manila package in front of them. They were all looking at Paul as he continued his directions.

"Inside each package, you will find explicit instructions on how to integrate the enclosed software with your respective operating systems. These instructions must be followed precisely. Any attempt to reverse engineer, or modify the software in any way, will activate a self-destruct mechanism in the software."

"I won't go into the details of what the software does and doesn't do. This is a matter of national security and you have absolutely no need to know what the software does. I will warn you, though, that each software package has built in defense mechanisms that are designed to make sure that the software is not modified, or even viewed. If your release is damaged, inadvertently or otherwise, you must contact us immediately for a replacement."

"Are there any questions?"

One of the personal computer company representatives addressed Paul. "Dr. Sanders, our operating system has been around for a long time, and the internal commands are regularly modified by the users. What effect will be seen if the user attempts to modify the operating system commands."

"That's an excellent question. We have anticipated your users' requirements to modify the operating system to a limited degree. There is virtually no way that they will be able to discover the software once it is integrated into the system. However, if they inadvertently corrupt the software the operating system will become inoperable, and your user will have to reload the system from the original distribution media. The requisite text additions to your manuals are also included in your packets."

Another representative addressed Paul. "Dr. Sanders, when do you want this disseminated, and how are you going to insure that the changes have been made?"

"That is also covered in your information packets. There is also a press release to be sent out by each company and an upgrade letter to be sent to each user. Each letter is somewhat different, as is the release timetable. We are trying to avoid any semblance of a mass change of operating systems by all vendors at the same time. I won't go into the details of the plan. You each have a role to play and that role is all that you need to know. This is for your own good, as well as for the good of the project."

The representative for a large mainframe computer company addressed Paul, anger rising in his voice. "Dr. Sanders, this is preposterous. Our customers cannot afford to lose their operating systems because of some mistake. The reloading of the operating system is quite complex."

Paul narrowed his gaze and addressed the representative directly. The anger which he had internalized for so long peeked out cautiously, punctuating his reply and giving it a power that was beyond argument. "We face a national emergency. Your customers will be far more inconvenienced if they have their data destroyed and their operation halted completely. Believe me, your insolent attitude offends me. People are dying because of this problem. You gentlemen have neither the motive nor the capability of stopping this problem. Had you had the foresight to deal with this problem, we would not have had to take the drastic actions we are now forced to rely upon."

As he finished his last sentence Paul looked around at all the representatives. He bore the look of a man not to be trifled with. His steely gaze made it clear to those representatives that Paul Sanders was not going to take flak from anyone.

The representatives avoided Paul's glare. His reprimand voiced the unspoken thoughts of every man in the room. There was no profit in developing virus proof operating systems, and thus no vendor had ever taken the initiative of putting some sort of safety precautions into their operating systems. As a result, some 700 people had been killed, hundreds more injured, and the entire national computer infrastructure was in jeopardy.

There were no further questions after Paul's response to the mainframe vendor.

Each representative took his distribution package and moved out of the room solemnly. Some even took time to shake Paul's hand and thank him for his handling of the matter.

After the last representative left, Paul sat down wearily in his chair. He closed his eyes and rubbed his temples slowly, praying that the pressure he had endured for so long, would soon be relieved. JAGERMEISTER was their only hope for quickly removing the

ENCHANTRESS virus from every computer, without human intervention. The alternative scenario was unthinkable.

If JAGERMEISTER did not solve the problem, then random acts of violence might continue for years, even if Randall and his team found the terrorists and stopped them from mutating the virus. If the terrorists suspected that JAGERMEISTER existed, and mutated the virus before they were caught, then COMPOPS would have to start all over again.

With these thoughts in his mind, Paul prayed to God that all would go well. He finished his silent meditation, walked across the room, and turned out the lights.

Everything was in motion.

It was time to sit back and watch the game.

May 28, 21:30 MDT

Jasmina was working on a set of instructions for a computer system that controlled the Bay Area Rapid Transit system. ENCHANTRESS had brought the system under it spell, and had let the NECROMANCER know of her success.

ENCHANTRESS had general instructions that were capable of disabling or killing certain computers, but the real beauty of the ENCHANTRESS virus, was its ability to execute specific commands that the NECROMANCER might give, to achieve a desired result, Jasmina and several other programmers worked feverishly to plan and write these specific commands, and to communicate them back to the enchanted computer systems.

Suddenly, Ibn was behind Jasmina. He interrupted her work by quietly clearing his throat. Jasmina turned around and saw that Ibn looked even more serious than usual. "What is it Ibn?,"she asked, trying to conceal her anxiety.

"We just got word from one of our operatives in Seattle. It seems that there is an unexpected operating system upgrade being worked on. He hasn't gotten all of the details, but the regular upgrade that was due in three months, is being interrupted for this intermediate upgrade."

Jasmina knew what was implied. Still it was inconceivable to her that counter measures could have been developed so rapidly.

The news caught her totally off guard.

Evan Smith's unfortunate, but necessary demise had lulled her into the belief that she would not have to mutate the ENCHANTRESS for quite some time. "Are you sure that this has anything to do with the ENCHANTRESS?," she asked. "After all, one operating system change is not unusual."

"We have collateral intelligence that shows that several other operating systems are being readied for upgrades. The schedules are staggered, but the possibility that this is in response to ENCHANTRESS cannot be ignored. It's time for you to start the mutation Jasmina. We don't want to lose the initiative."

Jasmina sighed. The long hours and limited resources had taken their toil upon Jasmina and her team of programmers. They worked in shifts around the clock to keep up with flood of information that ENCHANTRESS sent to them. They had not been able to write specialized code for even a hundreth of the computer systems that had come under the spell of ENCHANTRESS. Now even that limited effort would have to be halted as the entire team worked to mutate ENCHANTRESS and get the new version of the spell to all the computers before the operating systems changes.

Jasmina brushed her dark hair off of her forehead and took a deep breath. "Okay Ibn, I'll call the team together and start working on the mutation. Do you want us to finish our ongoing assignments before we start?"

"How long till you finish them?"

"No more than 12 hours, tops. Some of the team will be done before that so we'll be available to start the mutation within the next couple of hours."

"Good, go ahead then and finish the ongoing work. No more new targets will be started though, until the virus has been mutated and released."

Jasmina nodded and turned back to her console. She immediately contacted the other members of her team who were currently working. They would inform the other members of the team as they came on duty. She then returned to her instructions for the BART commuter system.

As Jasmina finished her conversation with Ibn, a C130 flying at an altitude of 30,000 feet let loose its load of men. This exercise was known as HALO, High Altitude Low Opening, and was designed to avoid detection by even the most alert of enemies. Hawkins followed his team out the door and dropped for what seemed like an eternity.

Hawkins loved jumping. It was the closest thing to sex you could do with your clothes on. HALO was the best of the best.

Most airborne troops only jump using static lines. This was the safest and most efficient way to drop large amounts of troops. In a static line drop, the parachute is opened automatically after the jumper clears the plane. Once the chute is open, the paratrooper is left to the whims of the elements and is greatly exposed to enemy fire. Because of this, static line drops are done from relatively low altitudes.

HALO requires exiting the airplane at much higher altitudes. Many times the jumpers must wear oxygen masks to breath at the elevations they drop from. HALO jumpers cannot pull their chutes at the extremely high altitudes they jump from, or it would take an extremely long time to reach the ground. Instead HALO jumpers free fall until they reach the lowest altitude at which they can safely pull their chutes and slow their rate of descent sufficiently before reaching the ground.

Hawkins moved into a position known as max track. This position literally turned the skydiver's body into a bullet and insured the fastest possible rate of descent. He watched the altimeter mounted on top of his reserve chute. The dial on the altimeter reached the red area indicating that it was time to pull the rip cord. He pulled the cord and felt the black silk chute claw into the sky. He immediately looked up to make sure that the airfoil had deployed completely and that none of his lines were tangled.

Assured that his main chute had performed properly, Hawkins now focused his attention on the rapidly approaching terrain below. The members of the team would rendezvous at the edge of a clearing about 5 miles from where the satellite communications had been located. Hawkins was going over the operations plan in his mind as he maneuvered his chute to avoid a large clump of pine trees. He readied himself for the impact, bringing his legs together so that they worked in conjunction as he landed.

The airfoil design of the chute allowed the skydivers to land gently. This was yet another advantage to HALO jumping. The circular, non-steerable chutes of regular paratroop units required that the jumper brace himself for a severe impact. Broken legs and sprained ankles were *de riguer* in regular airborne jumps. These casualties were acceptable when dropping large amounts of men. When there were no replacements, though, every jumper needed to land in one piece and so Delta and other specialized units used the more expensive, but far more maneuverable airfoil chutes.

Hawkins stepped to the ground and released the steering lanyards that were attached to the risers. The chute deflated and Hawkins moved quickly to secure the chute. One of the biggest dangers was that of being drug by one's chute. Hawkins quickly captured the silk, took off his rig and covered it so that it could not be discovered. He quickly consulted his compass and determined where he was. He looked at his watch, the luminous dial said 2130. He figured that he could make the rendezvous point in 30 minutes. He tightened the straps on his backpack and took a bearing with his compass before starting off.

As he started off he started contacting his team members via his radio headset. He decided not to use his night vision gear. Instead he would rely on his own night vision and superior training. Hawkins liked to keep his skills honed, and found that reliance on the technological marvels could make a person go soft.

In this business soft was definitely NOT good.

May 28, 22:00 MDT

Hawkins rendezvoused with his team at 2155. He immediately dispatched two members of the team down to a point near the road so that they could coordinate with the FBI and army assets who were bringing the support equipment. The remainder of the team moved with Hawkins in a wide search pattern toward the location of the satellite dish. They were careful not to make a sound as they traversed the terrain.

Moving noiselessly at night is no small feat for a human being. It takes a great deal of training and patience to learn how to move with stealth in the dark. As man's primary sense, sight, diminishes, the senses of hearing and smell struggle to fill the information void. The sound of a twig snapping, rocks moving, or leaves crushing under foot, become easily distinguished once sight is repressed.

Despite this Hawkins and his men moved through the darkness with nary a sound. They occasionally keyed their mikes to indicate to the other team members that they had detected something. When someone keyed their mike, the entire team halted immediately. They were all poised and ready to strike, determined to pay their enemies back for the Chlorine Catastrophe, for lock-in, and for having to jump into the God-forsaken mountains when they could be back at Ft. Bragg.

Hawkins caught a whiff of smoke, he immediately keyed his mike and issued curt orders. The team paused. The men on the right and left flanks began a circular searching pattern. They moved even more cautiously and tried to locate the source of the odor.

Hawkins heard Johnson, the man on the left flank as he quietly reported that he had found a ventilation shaft a few meters in front of him.

Hawkins consulted his topographical map to ascertain if there was supposed to be any such shaft in the area. He saw that there was an abandoned uranium mine in the area.

Hawkins quietly signaled the left half of his team toward the entrance to the mine and instructed Johnson to join them. He then took the other half of his team and moved to locate the satellite dish.

Both groups moved up the mountain. Johnson's half of the team reached the mine shaft entrance and quickly established a perimeter that allowed coverage of the area without detection. It was obvious that the mine was being used as the base of operations. There were vehicles secreted around the mine entrance and guards stationed around the mine.

Hawkins and the part of the team that remained with him, moved onto the area of the satellite dish. Someone keyed their mike and the team halted. One of the members on the right flank spotted the dish and a couple of guards around it. Hawkins left a rear guard and moved the rest of the team far enough back down the hill to establish a secure base of operations. Hawkins immediately had his radioman set up their own satellite communications link with Randall.

"Bravo Sierra, this is Lima Sierra, over."

Randall was drinking a cup of coffee and staring at the long dark stretch of road when he heard Hawkins' call come through the radio in the back of the HMMWV. The radioman answered and then passed the mike to Randall. "How's it going Hawkins, did you find the perps?"

Hawkins laughed to himself, he was used to thinking in terms of enemies and Randall was used to thinking in terms of perpetrators. "Roger, Bravo Sierra, we have secured the main entrance and the other item. I've relayed instructions to the forward team to meet you and direct you to the staging area. We're going to sack out for now. I've got some men reconnoitering for alternative exits from the base, our maps don't show any other exits, but I want to be sure."

Randall was elated. He had hoped from the outset that the Delta team would locate the terrorists quickly. He finished talking to Hawkins and then got on the convoy frequency. "This is Bravo Sierra, we are going to accelerate convoy speed to 70. I say again, convoy speed to seven zero."

Several amazed replies came back, but no one hesitated to accelerate to the suggested 70 miles per hour. The convoy streaked across the dark New Mexico evening, heading for the culmination of a journey that had started all the way across the country in New York.

May 29, 03:00 MDT

Randall rested for a while as the convoy rolled on. They reached Hawkins' men and headed quietly for a spot close to the mine entrance. The spot was well hidden and far enough away so that the noise would not carry to the terrorist's patrols

When everyone was in position. Randall made a secure phone call to Paul Sander's back in Maryland. After making the call Randall made some last minute arrangements and stood everyone down. He knew that the long drive and flight had zapped his people. They had waited this long and could wait a few more hours to make sure that no one made a stupid mistake because of fatigue.

May 30, 06:00 EDT

Dave was starting his day early. It was 6 AM and he had just hung up the phone with some of his staff in California. They had been trying to identify and clean up all of the infected computer systems which had been flooding the Federal Reserve system with bad message traffic. As he turned to his computer to write a memo, his phone rang again. He sighed heavily and picked up. "Anderson here."

"Dave, it's Paul. Sorry to bother you, but I just got a call from some people that need you in New Mexico."

"New Mexico, what the hell is in New Mexico?"

"Could be the end of our problems. I can't tell you anymore than that."

"You'll have to meet the guys out there to learn anything else. Basically, you need to be at the heliport in about an hour. The helicopter will take you to Andrews, where you will take a military jet to Kirtland Air Force Base in New Mexico. Depending on how things go while you are in the air, you may or may not get on a helicopter right away for your final destination. Let's hope your layover isn't long."

"Jeez, too bad the Military Airlift Command doesn't have a frequent flier program. I think I'd have a couple of first class tickets to Tahiti by now."

"I know Dave, I really feel bad about doing this to you on such short notice. It's just that since we lost Evan, you're the most knowledgeable person on this project."

"I always wanted to be on the fourth floor. Now I wish I'd never heard of it."

"You don't mean that Dave. We're finally seeing the light at the end of the tunnel. Oh, by the way, you'll be meeting with an outside consultant at Kirtland. He's been briefed on everything and is cleared for all levels of COMPOPS. Use him as much as possible."

"We'll do boss. Anything else?"

"Yeah have fun out there, see the sights. Bring me back one of those Navajo Kuchina dolls."

Dave laughed. "Sure boss anything for you."

Dave hung up the phone and proceeded to write his memo. The Federal Reserve problem had been solved temporarily by stopping all traffic from infected nodes. This was only a stop gap measure until the code Dave and Evan had written could be used to disinfect the enchanted systems. Dave did not know about the JAGERMEISTER project, but a non-virulent "virus disinfectant" had been given to Dave and his team. This non-virulent version simply cleaned up an infected computer system. It would not protect the system from further infection.

Because of the COMPOPS charter, Dave never even considered suggesting that a virulent version of the ENCHANTRESS disinfecter be developed. He knew that the lines had been drawn and that to suggest crossing those lines might well bring an abrupt end to his new and aspiring career. This left Dave with the huge task of guiding his team through the disinfection of literally thousands of infected computers. It was a formidable task to say the least.

It was with these thoughts in mind, that Dave composed the memo on his computer. It was a detailed plan for establishing rapid response teams for the extermination of viruses that popped up. He realized that the logistical problems involved in combating the virus as it popped up, would soon stretch the capabilities of his meager staff to the breaking point.

Dave quietly blamed the developers of the many computer operating systems and software for not developing an industry wide standard for integrity checking to thwart viruses. Several different algorithms and mechanisms had been developed which could stop virus infection, yet not a single vendor provided inherent protection against validation of software integrity.

Dave finished his memo and made a couple of calls to his teams. He then called Alan Foster. Alan was the most senior Alpha team member on the project and had been designated as Dave's backup when Dave had to travel. "Alan, Paul just called me and gave me travel orders. I don't know when I'll be back."

"Okay Dave, anything I should know about in particular?"

"No, the teams are disinfecting the identified platforms. Just ride shotgun and watch for any anomalies. Guess I'll see ya when I see ya"

Dave hung up the phone and went to the corner of the office where he had a small travel bag packed. He had learned to keep a kit packed after the first time he had been tagged to travel on short notice. That had been the NYSE problem. He took one last look at the office, turned off the light, and headed for the helipad, wondering what the hell was in New Mexico.

May 30, 10:00 MDT

At about the same time that Dave was over Kentucky, Hawkins' surveillance team was reporting what they had learned so far about the size and status of the terrorist base. Hawkins released the team to rest and he headed back toward Randall's base of operations to pass the information on.

Hawkins approached the base carefully. He was spotted by one of the regular Army guards stationed around the perimeter, only because Hawkins wanted to be spotted. The guard asked for the password and then had Hawkins approach within 10 paces. He then made Hawkins place his identification on the ground and back away from it. The guard moved cautiously toward the ID and checked it. Hawkins was impressed with the guard's performance. Once the guard was satisfied with Hawkins' *bona fides*, he allowed Hawkins to pass.

"Where can I find Agent Randall?"

"He's over there in the command HMMWV."

Hawkins moved toward the HMMWV. It had a camouflage net over the top of it. The net was slanted outward toward the terrorist base so that an observer coming from that direction would not be able to detect it. Given the nature of the threat this was an acceptable set up.

Hawkins could see Randall through the windshield. He was sleeping in the passenger seat of the vehicle. Hawkins moved around the HMMWV and knocked quietly at Randall's door. Randall woke sleepily and turned to see Hawkins' grinning face. Randall opened the passenger door.

"What are you so happy about?"

"I was just thinking about how nice it must be to be able to sleep in while all of us peons do the real work."

Randall looked at his watch. It was ten o'clock, six hours since he had shut his eyes to rest. "I need my beauty rest," Randall croaked, half-smiling.

Randall stirred and stretched his body. He got out of the vehicle and took a deep breath. He started coughing immediately, "My god, what is that smell?"

"Fresh air," Hawkins answered. "Guess you city slickers don't get much of that do you?"

"I don't know, seems dangerous to me. How you gonna get all your daily nutrition if you can't breathe it?"

Hawkins laughed quietly. "Listen boss, we've got the forward intelligence on the bad guys' hideout. Thought we might want to put a plan together. The quicker we stop these guys, the quicker that we can all go home."

Randall started to gain his wits. The long hours had taken their toll. The convoy ride out, added to the long plane ride, had helped to tear him down more. He drew from his reserve strength and started to become revitalized. He and Hawkins headed toward the small mess area and got large cups of coffee and K-rations. They then headed back to the command vehicle and moved into the back, where they could go over the topographical maps of the area as they planned.

May 30, 18:00 MDT

The flight to Kirtland had been long, but not uncomfortable. The small executive aircraft that the Air Force had allocated to him had all the amenities. He traveled in comfort and read the latest Tom Clancy novel to pass the time. Clancy's work had immediately caught the attention of those who worked in the intelligence community. His insight into the workings of the inner sanctums of intelligence had amazed everyone.

Dave remembered talking to Evan about Clancy's books. Evan had been an avid fan of the author and had gotten Dave interested in them too.

Dave missed Evan. It had been a total shock to him when he had learned of Evan's death. Evan had been affable, understanding, and genuinely concerned for the well-being of those with whom he worked. Evan had been a true leader and Dave hoped that he could learn to be as skilled as Evan in matters of leadership as well.

Dave finished the seven hundred and some odd pages, just as the aircraft was making its approach into Kirtland. The plane touched down and taxied to a small hanger at the far edge of the field. Dave could see that there was a security detail posted around the building. They looked like they were with the same group as the guys that were sitting in the cabin of the plane with Dave. Dave referred to them as his shadows. They really didn't intrude into his life at all. He barely realized that they were around. Still, he knew that if there was an attempt on his life, they would be there in full force.

He wondered what had happened to Evan's security team. He knew that they had been there when he had been killed. They had even killed the son of a bitch who had shot the RPG at Evan's car before the terrorist could make sure that he'd killed Evan by spraying his body with automatic weapon fire. Still that part had not made sense. He knew that his security team would not allow him to be exposed to any kind of risk.

Dave cleared his mind of the thoughts about Evan's death. It was still a painful memory and Dave needed to stay focused on the job at hand. The aircraft stopped and the door opened. Dave's shadows exited the plane and talked briefly with their counterparts. When they gave Dave the all clear, he exited the jet and moved with his shadows to the small hangar. One of the guards opened the door for him and let him enter the building.

It took Dave a few seconds to adjust his eyesight to the relative darkness of the interior of the building. The bright New Mexico sun was something Dave was unaccustomed to, working as he did all day with computers. He thought for a minute that he was hallucinating, the visage which shone at him from across the room was surely a mirage caused by the intense heat and light of the New Mexican climate.

"Dave, you look like you've seen a ghost."

The voice sent cold chills down his back. It couldn't be, but it had to be.

"Evan?," Dave asked quietly, unbelievingly. "Evan is that you?"

"Well it sure as hell ain't a ghost buddy."

"You son of a bitch. I thought you were dead and all this time you've just been taking a vacation," replied

Dave fighting back the emotions that were flooding over him.

Evan moved across the room and gave Dave a warm embrace. Dave fought to choke back tears. He could scarcely believe that Evan was here. He had been at Evan's funeral just days ago and had said farewell to his friend. Evan's reappearance was no less startling than a true resurrection.

"What the hell's going on Evan? We just put you in the ground."

Evan smiled. "The rumors of my death have been greatly exaggerated. They didn't even come close when they tried to kill me. They almost killed one of my security team, though. The poor guy got a face full of flame and a body full of shrapnel but they got him stabilized at Johns Hopkins. The security team decided to use the attempt to their advantage and help make the trail cold, real cold."

"It doesn't get much colder than six feet under. It really is good to see you again Evan. Are you the 'contractor' that I was supposed to link up with."

"That's me bubba. I just got done talking to our interested parties and they've got a few lose ends to tie-up before they need us. Might as well grab a Coke and take it easy."

Dave and Evan sat in the hangar and caught up on events since Evan's demise, while they waited for the phone call beckoning them into the lions den.

"So do you know anything about who we're out here to help?," asked Dave.

"Yeah, FBI and the Army think they've located the outfit that is running this freak show. Our sister agency at Ft. Meade located the satellite uplink. They routed the link over to the safe house where I was stashed so we've had them shut down for a few days."

"You're kidding !"

"That's what I said when Paul stopped by and told me about it."

"So what are we doing here?:

"Basically waiting for the all clear. Paul doesn't want to take any chances. The NYSE thing was a close enough call. Seems they were going to hit you, me and anybody else they could get. Let's just say that we blew that Popsicle stand in the nick of time."

Dave was silent, he didn't realize how close he'd come to dying for his country. This definitely was not what he'd signed up for.

"You sorta left me holding the bag, Evan. While you been taken it easy I've. been working my ass off trying to beat this Federal Reserve thing."

Evan just smiled again. "Yeah, well I had the easy task of living like a caged rat and having to write a simulator to fool their commands to ENCHANTRESS before they decided to mess with another system."

May 30, 22:00 MDT

Hawkins and Randall worked most of the morning on an OP plan. When it was complete they briefed the section leaders and told everyone to stand down until midnight. The plan would take place at 2:00 am. It was a proven fact that this was the time at which the human mind was least aware, even in combat. The Delta teams were well versed in the psychological aspects of offensive operations.

The plan was for the Delta teams to silently move their way through the different layers of defense. They would quietly subdue the sentries as they moved further into the mine shaft.

Randall had been told that the satellite dish was not critical and that all that need be done was to take out the guards. Randall didn't understand why the dish didn't need to be taken out. He wasn't "cleared" for that information. He just prayed to God that there wouldn't be a repeat of the Chlorine Catastrophe, possibly on a much grander scale.

May 31, 02:00 MDT

Hawkins insisted on leading the first team. He wanted to avenge the dishonor that had been placed upon his team because of the Chlorine Catastrophe. He knew that his team was not totally responsible for the incident. They had not been the ones who had overlooked the telephone lines which had let the deadly cry for revenge escape. But the fact that it had happened on their shift was an insult to Hawkins' team all the same.

As he approached the first sentry at the mine shaft entrance, he took extreme pleasure in cold cocking the son of a bitch and catching the body before it could make any noise at all. Hawkins had a good feeling about this operation. "Payback is a bitch," he thought to himself.

Hawkins' partner took out the second sentry at precisely the same time that Hawkins was cold cocking the other one. The two then moved silently toward the entrance after making sure that the guards were firmly restrained and out of the way.

They moved through the shadows of the mine with stealth. They had not been able to ascertain what types of alarms would be inside so they had come prepared to meet any challenge. Their night vision lenses had adapters fitted to them which would show any kind of infrared or ultraviolet sensing devices. They scanned the walls and floors for mechanical traps and trip wires.

As the first team moved into the entrance of the mine shaft the second team took up positions outside of the mine. A third team took the two SLP sentries away from the mine area for interrogation. There was no time for intimidation, so drugs would he used immediately. Anything that was divulged to the interrogators about security or alarms would be passed immediately back to the Delta team as it transited the mine shaft.

The sentries at the satellite dish were taken out at the beginning of the operation as well. They too were hustled away to the interrogation team. The silence of the night was not disturbed by these nocturnal activities. The New Mexican wilderness embraced the hunters, aiding them in the pursuit of their prey.

Unlike the wilderness, the mine shaft itself daunted the hunters. It held out false security by casting shadows and presenting various nooks and crannies. But the mine shaft was the prey's home. It existed to protect its inhabitants.

Hawkins froze. He could hear at least two different voices in low conversation. It was a second set of sentries. Hawkins motioned his partner and they both hit the floor quietly. He knew the guards would instinctively be looking at eye-level. Their attention level would be low because of the sentries posted outside.

Hawkins moved down the corridor like a viper posed to strike. He edged toward the sound. From the shadows he could see that the shaft opened up into a room. The guards were sitting on some mine cars facing Hawkins' direction. Hawkins quickly ascertained that there wasn't going to be an easy way to take these guys out. He keyed his mike and spoke a single phrase into the headset. There was a flurry of activity outside the mine. The codeword that Eric had spoken meant that the shit was about ready to hit the fan.

The team that took out the satellite dish sentries had moved down to the ventilation shaft. They checked the cover for booby traps and found one. They disarmed it and removed the cover to the shaft. They then attached their ropes to some nearby pines and began a cautious descent.

They heard Hawkins' code through their headsets, just as they neared the end of the shaft. Below them they could see a well lit room with communications equipment and computers. They immediately relayed this information to the others.

Randall was sitting on the edge of his chair in the command HMMWV. He was listening intently to the radio traffic and watching the progress of the teams on the status board. He closed his eyes and said a silent prayer for the safety of the Delta team and for the successful completion of the raid. He opened his eyes in time to hear the next transmission.

"Lullaby" came Hawkin's voice over the radio.

Randall breathed a sigh of relief. Hawkins and his partner had pulled something out of their bag of tricks to take out the sentries without compromising the operation.

Eric Hawkins was quickly moving toward the two downed guards. Both had been shot with blow-guns. The darts tipped in a paralyzing agent that had immediately coursed through the veins of the sentries. Hawkins and his partner quickly wrapped up the two sentries and moved them back into the shadows. The sentries were immediately injected with an antidote/tranquilizer that was meant to stop the effects of the paralyzing agent before it caused them to stop breathing.

Having deposited their human cargo in the shadows, Hawkins and his partner moved quickly back down the corridor and through the small room, using the mine cars as cover. They then continued their sojourn down the mine shaft toward the target.

Hawkins knew that the team in the ventilation shaft was waiting for him to catch up with them. It was better to have a two pronged attack to insure the successful seizure of the operations center. According to the reports there were five to seven individuals working in there. It would be extremely difficult for the two guys in the vent shaft to take out that many people without giving one of the bad guys a chance to initiate some sort of destruct mechanism.

Hawkins came to a branch in the tunnel. He sent his partner off to check out the side tunnel. A couple of minutes later he received a report that the sleeping quarters were at the end of the side shaft. Hawkins immediately called up a replacement for his partner and dispatched three other individuals to support the apprehension of the terrorists who were in the sleeping quarters.

Eric and his new partner headed down the main tunnel, followed by four more Delta team members. They were close now. Eric could feel it. He slowed his team and motioned for caution. Now he could see a strong source of light. The team doffed their night vision devices and readied their weapons.

Eric and the other lead individual readied their stun grenades. Eric spoke another word into his microphone, "Gabriel."

At the sound of the word "Gabriel" the team in the vent shaft readied their weapons and stun grenades.

Again Eric went to the ground, as did the other lead team member. They approached the operations center.

When he was within five feet of the of the main room he stopped. He took a deep breath and whispered one last word into his head set

"Michael."

Five seconds after the last word was whispered, two stun grenades went off in the entrance way. As those grenades went off, so did grenades in the sleeping quarters Jasmina thought that there had been some sort of mine collapse. She couldn't see and her ears were ringing. As she tried to regain her senses, the vent shaft cover fell to the floor and the Delta team that had been waiting there, descended rapidly to the ground. Hawkins and the five other Delta team members in the tunnel rushed in.

Jasmina realized what was going on and reached for a red button beside her desk. Eric saw her movement. His orders were very explicit. He quickly fired a subsonic round that forced Jasmina's body away from the button, while removing half of her beautiful dark skinned head.

Death was instantaneous.

Ibn saw Jasmina fall and screamed as he reached for an Ingram MAC-10. He had adored Jasmina for her beauty, her devotion to the faith, and for her extreme brilliance. These infidels would pay for her death.

As he raised the weapon three subsonic rounds impacted within a split second of each other. He fell dead, the MAC-10 clattered across the floor.

Eric surveyed the situation. There were two dead, and four more unconscious from blows dealt them by Delta team members. All the computer equipment was intact. "This is AVENGER ONE, situation contained."

A crackle came across their headsets. "This is AVENGER TWO, situation contained."

Randall breathed a sigh of relief. He looked upward and gave thanks to God that his prayers had been answered. After dispatching the explosive ordinance teams and other personnel. He picked up the secure phone and made a quick call.

"Yeah, this is AVENGER. Send down our guests, the party is over."

May 31, 03:30 MDT

Evan was sleeping as fitfully as could be expected. His dreams were troubled. The attempt on his life had hit him harder than he had let on to anyone, even the agency psychiatrist who Paul had insisted he see. Death's recent visit reminded Evan of his own mortality.

"Dr. Smith."

Evan awakened, startled, "What is it?"

"Dr. Smith, they've secured the area, sir. They want you down there as soon as possible."

Evan cleared his eyes and realized that it was the same man who had showed up on the doorstep the night before the attempt on his life, "You really specialize in messing up peoples sleep cycles, don't you?," Evan was smiling.

"Well sir, if our services are required, the protectee usually isn't sleeping well even before we show up."

"Yeah, I know what you mean," Evan replied. He forgot how long it had been since he had been able work on a normal schedule.

"Is Dave up?"

"Yes sir, I think he was headed toward the coffee pot last time I checked."

"That sounds good. Great, I'm up. Thank you."

Evan's shadow slipped out of the room as silently as he had entered it. Evan was amazed at how controlled the man's motions were. It seemed that there was absolutely no waste of energy in his movements, no awkwardness at all. Evan rose and dressed quickly. He headed out into the

233

main area of the hangar and saw Dave with a large mug of coffee in his hand.

"Sleep well?," Evan asked as he crossed the hangar floor.

"Like a log," Dave replied.

"Well I guess they must have been successful. Otherwise we wouldn't be up at this god awful time of the morning."

"I thought you Montanans were early risers, feed the cows, that sorta stuff."

Evan laughed. "Nope, my dad was a professor, earliest he got up was 8:00."

Dave and Evan finished their coffee and headed toward the helicopter which was warming up a few yards from the hangar. They boarded and the helicopter rose into the dark sky, headed for the mountains of western New Mexico.

May 31, 06:30 MDT

Hawkins and the rest of the Delta team involved in the operation were in debrief. Eric took a long swallow of the coffee in his canteen cup. They had just learned from the ordinance guys, that the button that Jasmina Qaafar had been going for had been wired to explosives designed to bring tons of mountain down upon the computer equipment and everyone in the tunnels.

Eric had reacted on instinct. It had not been the first time that he had been so close to death. He had stared it in the face on several occasions. His instincts had been to shoot, and he had.

A total of twenty-five terrorists had been taken alive. There had been only two casualties. Hawkins attributed that to the soft nature and the youth of the terrorists involved. Most had lived in the US for several years and had lost the animal instincts and intense devotion of more seasoned conventional Palestinian terrorists.

Hawkins had met and dealt with members of the PLFP, these SLP members were nothing but wet behind the ears kids compared to those guys. Still eh appreciated the fact that these "kids" had inflicted more fear, death and injury upon the citizens of the US than all of the actions of the PLFP combined, with their little push buttons and computer systems.

As the debrief was finishing, Eric heard the whine of choppers overhead. That would be their ride home. The team broke up and went to get their gear. Eric wandered over to Randall's HMMWV.

235

"Well Agent Randall, looks like the good guys win."

"I don't know who won this one. They did a lot of damage, and scarcely fired a shot."

"I know what you mean," Hawkins replied. "It sure isn't the kind of terrorism that we're used to dealing with."

"Me neither," Randall replied. "Me neither."

"You guys getting ready to head out?"

"Yeah, pick up our gear and head back to Bragg for some R&R."

"You guys deserve it. I just want you to know how much I've appreciated your help. You guys are great, really."

"Thanks Agent Randall, you didn't do so bad yourself. Sorta hard to shoot bad guys if you don't know who or where they are."

"We lucked out," Randall replied, knowing that Hawkins didn't realize how true that statement was.

"Welp, gotta get out here and back to the Pines," Eric said, as he extended his hand toward Randall.

Randall shook Hawkins' hand firmly.

This motley team had achieved the impossible in an extremely short time. They had come together and worked as an efficient well-oiled machine because of their professionalism.

It was a shame to break up such a team, but it was a relief as well. The crisis was almost over, there was no longer a need for the knowledge and skills the Delta team possessed. That in itself was a relief.

Evan and Dave passed Hawkins on their way to find Randall. As integral a part as each had played in stopping the terrorists, they didn't have the faintest idea of who the others were.

Randall recognized the two individuals coming toward him as two of Paul Sanders' people. He knew that they would be coming to insure that the computer equipment was intact and prepared for shipment.

"Well look what the cat drug in," Randall called, smiling at Evan and Dave. Evan and Dave beamed. They shook Randall's hand.

"I hear you guys had a pretty big party here," Evan commented.

"Yeah, we need you guys to go over the equipment and other material we found and arrange for its shipping back to wherever you guys come from."

Evan laughed. He realized what an integral part this man had played in stopping this operation, but realized that they knew nothing about COMPOPS except that they were the "computer guys."

Evan voiced his thoughts.

"Talk about compartmentalization, it's surprising how well we came together to beat this thing."

Randall smiled. "Yeah, I was just thinking the same thing. Guess the system works, huh?"

Randall looked up toward the mine shaft. "EOD has cleared all the explosives out of the tunnels, so I can arrange to have Mike Zvaboda take you guys up."

Randall left for a minute and found Mike who was busy coordinating the management of the "crime scene."

"Hey Mike, here's our two computer experts. Why don't you get them what they need and get them started."

"Sure G."

Mike checked Evan and Dave in, and gave them identification badges. They walked up to the mine shaft and entered. The tunnel lighting had been enhanced with the addition of several flood lights attached to tripods.

The entire mine had been searched for explosives and the Explosives and Ordinance Disposal (EOD) team was just finishing up their work.

As they approached the operations center Evan noted a couple of "shadows" making sure that no one entered without proper clearance. They checked Evan and Dave's badges against a list of authorized personnel and let them proceed. Unfortunately, Mike was not authorized into the operations center, neither was Agent Randall. Even the EOD teams had been scrupulously supervised while they searched the center for explosives, and removed them.

Evan made sure that no one would be allowed into the operations center while Dave and he were working, then said thank-you to Agent Zvaboda, and entered the large underground SLP operations center.

"Looks like your office," Dave commented.

"Yeah, look at this stuff, cross-compilers, manuals, satellite uplink equipment, pretty sophisticated stuff for a bunch of college kids."

Dave and Evan made sure that all of the computer related equipment, manuals, and notes were carefully placed in one large area of the room. They meticulously marked every diskette and computer with the COMPOPS computer virus marker, and an appropriate ID and case number identification. By the time they finished it was almost noon.

Evan and Dave went out into the bright sunlight and proceeded toward their helicopter. Evan talked briefly to the leader of the security team and then looked at Dave.

"Well, we're about done here. The security team will make sure that the stuff we marked gets back to the agency ASAP."

"Great, I can't wait to get back to tracking down ENCHANTRESS infections," Dave replied facetiously.

"Well, we'll just have to track them down as they pop up," Evan said. "We might see a lot less damage than you would expect. The really devastating things that they did had to be written and uploaded onto the target machines. Now that we've caught the bad guys, there isn't anybody to upload the malicious instructions."

"What happens if someone comes across the virus and learns how to make it do its tricks?"

"Chances are slim to none. The encryption routines, and the fragmented nature of the code makes it tough for even someone who KNOWS that it's there to tame the beast."

"We can't do any more Dave, you know our charter," Evan lied.

He hated not being able to tell Dave about the JAGERMIESTER project. He knew that it was better if Dave didn't know about it though. If the project was discovered, at least Dave's job would be safe.

Dave and Evan said goodbye to Randall and Zvaboda and made sure that all the material had been removed from the operations center. They then climbed aboard their helicopter and headed back to Kirtland where they took the executive jet back to D.C..

July 28, 08:00 EDT

It had been several weeks since the event filled journey to New Mexico. Things had worked out surprisingly well, Evan thought. JAGERMIESTER had been released successfully and a quick check of the environment showed a significant reduction in the number of infected systems.

Evan was glad that he had agreed to writing JAGERMIESTER. It had been the only sure way to remove the ENCHANTRESS. He knew that Dave's concerns about the virus proliferating had not been unwarranted. He had hated lying to Dave but compartmentalization was the rule of this business.

Evan had just taken a month off to visit his parents and explain to them as best he was allowed about his faked death. They had been extremely shocked and overjoyed that they had not lost their son. Evan and his family spent a great deal of time up at their cabin in the mountains. Computers were not allowed at the cabin, it was a family rule. Evan had needed the time off. He was now totally re-energized and ready to go back to work.

Evan was reflecting on his vacation as he opened the cipher lock outer door. As he entered the office he saw Paul talking to the receptionist.

"Raised from the dead, and none the worse for wear, eh, Dr. Smith?", Paul quipped.

Evan smiled. "Good to be back Paul."

"Good to have you back," replied Paul. "Listen I've gotta check on some lab work. I'll drop by and talk to you later."

Paul headed toward the internal elevator and turned his key to a special position which took him to an small unobserved lab located above the fifth floor. He exited the elevator and entered a code on the electronic panel next to the lab door. The door opened and Paul entered.

Inside the room was a single computer that was working actively. Paul checked the monitor connected to the computer. "ENCHANTRESS destroyed. ...JAGERMEISTER AWAITING INSTRUCTIONS," appeared on the screen.

Paul appreciated compartmentalization, it was the only way to insure national security. Evan never even suspected that a few extra modules had been added to JAGERMIESTER. The President had made it quite clear that an event like this should never happen again. So the self-destruct mechanism of JAGERMIESTER had been substituted with a module that allowed execution of specific computer instructions.

"No one would ever abuse JAGERMIESTER," Paul thought as he left the room, the computer working frantically to handle the hundreds of calls that it was receiving.

ABOUT THE AUTHOR

Robin Jackson was born and raised in Montana. He entered the Army as a Russian linguist and went on to learn about and love computers in his work in the military intelligence community. After leaving the Army, Jackson worked in the Supervisory Control and Data Acquisition (SCADA) industry, eventually building a successful consulting company in that field. After selling his company Jackson became an Internet pioneer, buying ownership of the first Web Hosting company in the State of Montana.

Jackson has received numerous awards for his classified and unclassified work and holds several computer certifications including CISSP, CompTIA Security+, Wetstone's Certified Hacking Investigator and Certified Steganography Investigator and the Cyberterrorism Defense Analysis Center DHS Sentinel Incident Response and Handling certification.

Jackson was a member of the Williams Twins Forensics team which won the Department of Defense's 2010 DC3 Forensics Challenge and the EC Council's International Civilian team award.